MARQUESS OF MENACE
LORDS OF SCANDAL

TAMMY ANDRESEN

Copyright © 2021 by Tammy Andresen

All rights reserved.

No part of this book may be reproduced in any form or by any electronic or mechanical means, including information storage and retrieval systems, without written permission from the author, except for the use of brief quotations in a book review.

❧ Created with Vellum

Keep up with all the latest news, sales, freebies, and releases by joining my newsletter!

www.tammyandresen.com

Hugs!

CHAPTER ONE

Hells bells, Dylan hated these sorts of parties.

Loathed them, actually.

To be honest, he didn't like anything that involved society or the *ton*.

Awkward, considering he was a marquess.

Dylan Amesbury, Marquess of Milton, leaned against the wall with his arms crossed as he watched a sea of dancers sway back and forth in front of him, his face set in an annoyed frown.

He much preferred to spend his time at his secret gaming hell, the Den of Sins, or at his boxing club, or to be absolutely clear, having his fingernails ripped off one by one.

He wasn't meant for this sort of life, never had been. A fact his family was often fond of reminding him.

In some ridiculous series of events, he had inherited the Milton title, which should have gone to his third cousin, Lord Henry James Marks. Then his second cousin, the Honorable Steven Winthrop. His older brother, Mr. William Amesbury, would have been better but no. For some odd reason fate had placed the title in his hands. Loaded to the gills with debt, he'd been given the title and all the responsibility of turning the blasted marquisate around.

Laughable, really because of all the men who might have inherited it before him, he was the absolute worst choice. He drank, gambled, and generally skirted through life barely keeping himself out of trouble. Well, serious trouble anyhow.

His mother had gone into fits when she'd realized that he'd become the marquess. And her parting words to him on her death bed were, "Try not to bring the family any more shame."

He let out a long breath, shaking his head.

Three girls nearby giggled as they snapped their fans over their mouths and made eyes at him above the fluttering instruments. It was February. How could they be hot enough to fan with such vigor?

He looked away again, not bothering to even feign interest in the debutantes.

It wasn't that he didn't like women, he liked them very much. Short ones, tall ones, curvy ones, brash ladies who swore like sailors, exotic beauties, and everyday hard-drinking women who liked a quick laugh and a bit of fun with an even quicker tumble. He'd even dallied with a few ladies of society. Widows were a personal favorite of his.

If there was one type he didn't go for, it was the giggling, covered-in-lace, fan-waving, marrying type.

More precisely, he didn't mind the giggles or the lace…just the marriage part.

He let out another long breath. The very idea of tying himself to one woman left him cold deep inside. He'd been meant for life of fun, leisure, and debauchery. It's all he'd ever been good at. Ask anyone in his family. They'd agree.

But he found himself drowning in ledgers, crop counts, and… marriage prospects.

The Den of Sins had actually helped reduce the mountain of debt he'd inherited. But he had two crumbling estates with villages that had largely been abandoned and fields that had ceased producing.

He'd attempted to think of other ways to right the title, but the only real asset he had to leverage at this point was…well…his looks.

Dylan had been born handsome. A fact he'd utilized to its fullest advantage for most of his life and one he'd use again now to repair the title and prove to his family that he was capable of doing something no one else had done in the past few generations: be a successful marquess.

He scrubbed a hand through his hair and heard one of the ladies sigh. Longingly.

He should ask one of them to dance.

But dread churned in his stomach. He couldn't do it.

Still, he'd have to introduce himself to one of the taffeta confections at some point. If for no other reason than he needed to discern which of these women had the largest dowry and would make for the best candidate to become a marchioness.

To a sham marquess.

Neither reared for the duty nor holding the necessary dignity for the position, he was sure to disappoint.

He looked back at the girls, picked the one with the most lace and ribbons in her hair and winked. It was the only metric he could think to choose one of them over the others.

He knew this was not how most titled lords went about courting. There were introductions and pretty words and formal dances and blah blah blah. But he didn't have the time or energy for such pleasantries.

The sooner he wed and repaired his finances, the sooner he could go back to his old life of drinking and gaming hells. Where he was comfortable. Where he excelled.

And it turned out that debutantes and working women had a great deal in common because all three ladies blushed and giggled, and the fans moved even faster.

Perhaps courting wouldn't be as awful as he'd imagined.

"Good evening, my lord." An older woman stepped in front of the three young ladies and gave him a smile, coquettish and obvious as she dipped into a curtsy. "I am Lady Price, and these are my daughters, Lady Judith, Lady Penelope and Lady…" He ceased listening.

Each of the girls dipped into a matching curtsy to their mother's as they lowered their fans. Judith's bow was awkward, Penelope's teeth were horse-like, and whatever her name was…just no.

But he stood there making polite conversation for what seemed like hours before another matron introduced herself and her daughters and then another and another.

Each more painful than the last.

Finally, not able to stand another moment, he slipped from the crowd that had developed around him and started toward the terrace. He needed air or a carriage to whisk him from this party to the nearest gentlemen's club or, better yet, the Den of Sins. Where men unabashedly participated in cursing and drinking and womanizing.

But just as he reached the doors, he glanced over and saw her. Miss Eliza Carrington.

Tall and statuesque, her dark brown hair was piled high atop her head. Her coiffure lacked the ribbon and lace of so many other girls, which only added to the appeal of the lush locks. Dark lashes fringed her large, warm eyes, making them extremely mesmerizing.

Her nose was small and straight, set off by high cheekbones and her mouth was so full and lush it made a man ache. He didn't allow his gaze to sweep down her body. He already knew that her full curves would set him off into a riot.

He'd met Eliza on two separate occasions. One, very proper. The wedding of his best friend, the Duke of Devonhall, to Eliza's sister, Isabella Carrington.

But the other time made him grin. It had been the least proper meeting of a proper girl that he could think of. Which meant it had been exceedingly fun. In addition, Eliza was nothing like the rest of these girls. She had spirit and spunk and…he stopped.

Eliza was a distraction. Nothing more.

Even now two men stood near her, both intent upon her while she hardly looked at either of them. She was a woman made to tease men.

Normally, he'd love to allow her to tease him, but he had a future to prepare for. She didn't have the connections or funds he required and he needed to leave her be.

Which was why he kept moving and headed out onto the terrace. Eliza Carrington was not the right woman for him. Nor was he the right man for her. She struck him as the sort that would see right through his wicked ways to the black heart he hid underneath.

Eliza watched the Marquess of Milton head out the doors. Cad.

To his friends, he was just Menace. An apt name.

The man was trouble.

Eliza knew when a man was best left alone. Too handsome by half, as near as she could tell, Menace had never worked an honest day in his life.

She gave an indelicate snort as she watched him walk out the doors.

"Don't make such noises, dear." Her Aunt Mildred patted her arm. "It isn't polite."

Eliza frowned at the other woman who wasn't actually her aunt. The truth was, she was an actress that Eliza and her sisters had hired to play the part of their real aunt. The actual Mildred hadn't left Scotland in twenty-five years, which made impersonating the lairdess exceedingly easy.

The why of the whole situation was a bit more complicated.

It started with her mother's death and her father's disappearance.

Her mother's death hadn't actually been the complicated part, which had been a standard case of disease of the lung. Funny how the mundane could be so heart wrenching. But their father, a merchant, had been on a trip to the Orient when she'd passed.

They'd made several attempts to contact him but to no avail. Lucas Carrington had neither returned home nor written to say when he might. It had been almost a year since they'd received any communication from him.

She covered her stomach as nerves raced along her skin. And their uncle, their mother's sister's husband, had had their father declared dead and seized any assets he could get his claw-like hands on.

Including Eliza and her sisters. Malcolm had tried to marry them off to whatever man would have them. More accurately, he wished to sell Eliza to the highest bidder to collect the purse, but her younger sister, Isabella, had met and married a duke. The Duke of Devonhall now had all four Carrington sisters under his protection.

Which was a blessing at this exact moment. Because her uncle stood next to her with the noxious Mr. Taber.

"Eliza," the man hissed as he reached for her arm, gripping her too hard. "I know you remember our friend, Mr. Taber."

Taber gave her a greasy smile, his eyes wandering all over her. "Miss Carrington." He stepped closer, the odor of him filling her nostrils and curling her nose. He stank of old cigar and body odor, his hair slicked back giving him a greasy appearance.

"Mr. Taber," she replied coolly. Her uncle had planned to marry her to this man before Devonhall had stepped in.

"I wondered if I might have the pleasure of a dance." His gaze travelled over her body again, lighting with greedy desire.

She shivered. Then he reached out a hand, his nails overly long in a way that made them resemble talons and touched her bare shoulder. She stepped aside. "Apologies, but my dance card is full."

Her uncle made a noise of dissent, tightening the hand of her other arm. "Then why are you standing here?"

"I am waiting for my escort, though you may have frightened him off," she replied, notching her chin higher. She refused to be intimidated by her uncle. He had no sway over her.

He yanked at her arm, causing her to lose her balance and lean closer. "Listen to me, girl," he hissed in her ear. "You may think that you can get away from me, but I am still your uncle and you'll do as I say."

"I won't," she fired back.

Mr. Taber sneered. "It's all right, Malcolm. I like a filly that needs to be broken."

That made her start. The words were so coarse and deep-down crass that she attempted to take a half step back. And Eliza never ran from anything.

But this man was dangerous and so was her uncle. Her stomach roiled as she considered the idea of intimacy with him. A shiver ran down her spine. She couldn't. She would not allow this man to touch her. Ever.

Eliza and Isabella had decided that the best way to keep all the sisters safe was to marry each of them to a respectable man and so they were attending every party they could gain an invitation to in order to officially enter the marriage mart.

As soon as her sisters were married…she'd be free of her uncle and his schemes forever.

Of course, in the meantime, partaking in society meant her uncle could easily find them. Her sister and new husband usually attended but they'd taken an evening for themselves. A miscalculation. Eliza would have to tell them that Devonhall needed to be with them at every event. She nearly sighed. Bash had taken on a great deal of responsibility when he married her sister.

She looked back at the Menace, clearly visible on the terrace.

Despite his title, the Marquess of Menace was not on the list of potential candidates. He was a man no respectable woman should marry.

Not that Eliza was all that respectable. In the period between her mother's passing and her sister's wedding, Eliza had done a great many things that would have ostracized her from society, but she regretted none of them. She'd do them all again to save her sisters.

She'd managed to keep her virtue but her innocence…that was long gone. She knew things about the world now and there was no going back.

"If you'll excuse me, Uncle. I see my escort." And then she yanked her arm, with a quick jerk, out of his grasp. Because she needed to escape this conversation.

And much as Eliza hated to admit it, Menace could help.

So as the fake Aunt Mildred patted her sister Emily's arm and pointed to a major she wished for Emily to meet, Eliza stepped backward and slipped out onto the terrace. Away from her scowling uncle and leering Mr. Taber. She'd die before she married that man.

Menace stood with his back to her, staring off into the darkness.

Even she had to admit that his shoulders were devilishly broad as he stood with his arms crossed.

His dark hair waved back from his face in a careless windswept look that highlighted his strong jaw and piercing green eyes. Not that she could see his features now. But the memory of them haunted her more often than she cared to admit.

She drew in a steadying breath, trying to decide where to begin. She looked back to see Mr. Taber still watching.

"What do you want, Eliza?" Menace asked, not turning to look at her.

She stopped, still several feet away. The cad. How had he known it was her? Still, she was strangely relieved to be out here with him and not in the ballroom still. "What are you doing here? I never see you at these sorts of events."

"Because I never come," he replied. Then he turned to look at her. A half wall flanked the terrace and he rested his lean hip against it, looking casual and masculine and rakishly handsome. "And you answered a question with a question."

"So I did," she murmured, moving closer again. But not too close. The man was distractingly appealing. He radiated the sort of heat that made her flush and he smelled like…leather and pine and male musk that scattered her thoughts. Rakes were so good at that. And he was the best. "I was hoping to ask you a few questions. Privately."

She heard him let out a sharp breath, his back straightening up. "No."

Drat.

Eliza suspected that her brother-in-law, the duke, had warned Menace to stay away from her. Which suited her just fine. She didn't need a rake making her already complicated life even messier. In fact, she'd like to avoid men and marriage all together.

Her sisters all had a rosy view of their parents' marriage, one that drew them to the union. But as the eldest, Eliza knew better. Her father had been gone for long stretches, casting most of the work onto her mother. Work her mother had then relied on Eliza to help complete.

The truth was, Eliza didn't need a husband and she wasn't sure she wanted one either. Not when she was perfectly capable of taking care of herself. But the sooner she got her sisters married, the sooner they'd be out of her uncle's clutches. "You don't even know what questions I might ask."

He shook his head. "I know exactly what questions you're going to ask. Ask them of your brother-in-law."

Eliza held in her huff of frustration. She had...multiple times. Bash, in a misguided attempt to protect her, kept telling her not to worry. The men were handling it. She didn't need to be coddled or protected, she'd been the protector her entire life. "Well, I'm going to ask you. Has anyone found any direct evidence of wrongdoing on my uncle's part?"

Menace grimaced as he turned to face her, his eyes wandering down her frame. She knew the look. Men often gave her such glances. The difference was the effect *his* had on her. Heat prickled along her skin.

"Besides when one of his henchmen shot Bash's driver?"

She stepped closer. "Thank goodness he recovered."

Menace shrugged. "I agree except the shooter swore it was an accident and where there was no death..."

She frowned. "No wrongdoing."

"Nope," he replied, leaning his backside against the wall and kicking out his feet. "I know he sold your house. But that's it and that was completely legal. Are we done now?"

She moved closer still, making certain to add a bit of sway to her hips. He noticed. "Nearly." She gave him her most angelic smile. The one she used when she needed something. "The mystery man who keeps appearing. Do we know who he is yet?"

A man had raced in and rescued her and her sisters when their uncle had attacked their carriage, but no one knew who he was. They did know that their father had a secret partner and they'd wondered if their mystery man was one and the same but so far, they'd gotten no proof.

"Why are you asking me all of this?" He gave her a level stare.

"Because," she started, then paused. She was close now, close enough to touch him. Her fingers flexed. She shouldn't want to reach out. She should only be calculating whether or not she should touch him to get the information she needed. "Bash is under the misguided impression that he needs to protect me."

Menace raised his brows. "How foolish."

"Exactly," she replied. "I don't need protection. I—"

"You practically threw your sister at him in order to gain his protection, if I recall."

He had her there. But Eliza had noticed the attraction between the two when she'd suggested her sister get involved with the duke. "Isabella did need help. Emily and Abigail need him too."

"But not you..." he murmured.

His voice had dropped so low the sound made her shiver. He's a rake, she reminded herself. "Not me."

"But you need my help now?"

Her chin notched up. "Not help. Just information."

He quirked a one-sided smile that did strange things to her insides as he let out a chuckle. "An important distinction to be certain."

"What is the harm in giving me a few facts?"

"I don't know you well enough to know if there is harm in it or not. You seem like you could be dangerous."

She raised one shoulder. Female pride coursed through her. "I take that as a compliment."

He pushed off the wall, which brought him closer to her body. So close that she could feel his heat. Her dress came off her shoulders exposing a fair bit of skin including her rather ample cleavage. Which was currently covered in goosepimples.

He brought his hand to her shoulder, large and warm, his fingers fanning out so that his pinky rested just about the swelling flesh of her right breast. She shivered at the touch despite herself.

He dropped his chin lower, angling his sharp green eyes to meet hers. "You shouldn't."

Eliza did what she knew she shouldn't. She'd manipulated a fair number of men, but none were as dangerous as this one. He was confident, in control, and he made her forget her principles every time he drew near. Still, she moved closer, allowing her breasts to just graze his chest. "There must be some way I could convince you."

CHAPTER TWO

Minx.

Dylan stared down at Eliza. Her eyes tilted at the corners, giving them an almond shape that could make a man beg. He'd like to beg...

Her lips were softly parted, and the brush of her skin made him hard and hot.

She knew exactly what she was doing.

"What are you offering?" If she wanted to play this game, he'd see her bluff and raise her. He owned a gaming hell after all.

The softest sweetest smile lifted the corners of her mouth. "Let me think. I want regular updates about what's happening in my own life. And you want..." She paused, raising one of her hands and brushing a finger on the plump flesh of her bottom lip.

His trousers grew achingly tight. This woman was going to be his undoing.

Dylan had dallied with a few of society's elite. He didn't discriminate when it came to women. The only exception was marriageable maidens.

But Eliza had been without a chaperone for months. Had she been with a man? Her demeanor certainly suggested she had. She knew things. Things a debutante should not.

And he'd take her up on her offer in a second. Hell, he'd pull her into the shadows and lift her skirts right here if he thought he could get away with it but...Bash would kill him.

Then again, might be the way to go. The title and all its debt could go to the next cousin while he died doing what he loved best. "I want —" he started, wrapping a hand about her waist and pulling her body tight against his.

"My lord," she softly purred. "Someone might see." She glanced over her shoulder, scanning the room.

He relaxed his hold, easing back. She was right.

She placed her hands lightly on his chest. "I'm offering information in return."

He gave her a confused stare, as his brows drew together. That was not at all what he'd expected. "Information? What knowledge could you possibly give me?" Her tongue darted out, licking along her top lip. He followed the movement, his brain barely working.

"Let me think. You're here, even though you've never come to one of these parties before. What's more, you were flirting with those ninny heads, surrounded by debutantes. That can only mean one thing. You're looking to marry."

He startled and took a step back, bumping his legs into the rock wall behind him. "How did you..." But he couldn't finish. She'd taken him completely off guard.

She rolled her eyes, stepping back. "Please. I can read you like a book."

Wait? Had she just been pressing against him in invitation or had she been manipulating him? "Did you just brush against me because you were offering me..." He trailed off again. He wasn't usually at a loss for words, but tonight, he just couldn't seem to make them come out.

"I am offering to help you if you help me," Eliza quipped. "I have spent the last month learning every lord and lady and who has influence and who has money."

His jaw dropped down and he snapped it closed again. "So why touch me?" If he were being honest, his pride had been wounded.

He'd thought for a moment she wanted him as much as he desired her.

One of her brows quirked. "You're awfully fixated on that."

Because it had been delightful. His mind had become blank as… Damn. "You did it on purpose."

"You were being very resistant."

He shook his head. "You're a she-devil. A curse to men," he hissed.

She shrugged. "I just happen to understand the male mind. Not that it's difficult. Which is why I know what you're doing here. And how you need help."

He scrubbed the back of his neck. "How is that?"

"Let me think. You're looking for a wife. Not because you wish to marry. I know your type." She tapped her chin. "Is it money or connections? I'm guessing money."

Minx. A wave of frustration washed over him. He wished she were wrong. It disconcerted him how right she was. "So you're suggesting that I keep you in the loop and in return, you help me with my search."

"Exactly."

He shook his head. Every part of him warned him against her proposal. "Besides the fact that Bash would actually end my life, and the information could be dangerous for you. You are the last woman who should be helping me to find a bride."

"Why?" Her chin notched up again and he had the urge to run a finger along her jaw. Trace its outline and test the texture of her skin. Was it as silky as he imagined?

"Because you are far too smart and far too beautiful."

To his complete amazement, she blushed. It might have been the most honest and vulnerable thing she'd done since he'd met her, and it stole his breath how stunning she looked with her cheeks stained, a pale pink that only enhanced her coloring. "Thank you." She swallowed, her eyes casting toward the ground. She crossed a hand over her front, grabbing the other arm. She'd gone from confident to vulnerable in a moment and he wondered if this was a trick again. But the tremble in her voice told him she meant her next words. "I've worked very hard to keep my sisters safe. I can't just turn the feeling off that I need to protect them. I need to know what's happening. Bash has been wonderful, and he wants to help but…"

He understood. "There is no word on the mystery man."

"Will you tell me if you learn anything?"

Maybe. Probably not. "I'll consider it. Now…" He drew up. "I've given you two important bits of information. Point me in the direction of a rich and eligible young woman."

She gave a single nod. "See the punch bowl? There is a lady in a particularly interesting shade of tangerine orange."

He looked over to the far side of the ballroom. Sure enough there was a girl in layers of orange lace and piles of matching hair ribbons. "I see her."

"She's the Earl of Westerly's daughter. Richest man in England. Lady Carmella Dumbly."

He swallowed. She was exactly the sort he was looking for and she was absolutely awful. Even from here, he hated her dress, her hair, the exaggerated way she drew attention to herself.

He looked down at the classic beauty in front of him. Eliza was the sort of stunning good looks mixed with intelligence and grit that could melt a man like him. And yet…she wasn't for him. He'd have to repeat that a hundred more times before this ball was over.

Eliza wasn't for him.

"Our bargain is done," he said and then he walked away. Toward Lady Carmella Dumbly.

Eliza watched Dylan cross the room with her head held high. But inside, she shrank a bit. She'd just taken some big risks to learn very little.

Her uncle was forcing her hand. Drat the man.

She'd practically offered herself to a rake. In her defense, she had no intention of actually allowing him liberties. But that didn't mean it had been a good idea. Women had been ruined for less.

She'd just been looking for a way to slip past his defenses and get what she'd needed from him.

Information.

She sighed as she watched him slide next to Carmella. Instantly he drew the girl's attention away from the other men surrounding her. Eliza allowed herself another long sigh as she slipped back into the ballroom. Of course he had. The man was distractingly dashing.

There had been a moment where she'd brushed up against him that she'd nearly forgotten herself. She'd wanted to slide her arms up around his neck and touched her lips to his.

She shook her head. Despite her bluff that she had all sorts of experience, in truth she had very little. And a rake was no man from whom to learn such things.

She didn't want to marry so she was less worried about her own reputation, but her sisters needed to wed, and she'd not allow a foolish crush on a rake to ruin their futures.

Once they were taken care of…she shrugged. Perhaps she'd never go near a man again. Or perhaps she'd take to the stage and become an actress, or mayhap she'd travel to America and visit the wild west.

She laughed despite herself.

Such adventures sounded exciting and a welcome change from worrying and work. Not that Eliza regretted caring for her sisters. She loved them more than anything. But once they were safely matched and her mother and father's assets were back in her hands, the world was her oyster.

Her gaze darted to Menace again. Somehow, Carmella was already hanging off his arm as though he were the most fascinating man in all of England.

Perhaps he was.

Eliza would never admit this to anyone, but she might find him fascinating as well. She'd lied when she'd said he was simple. He was such a mystery that he sometimes stole her breath. How could one man create such a riot inside her body?

The warm air of the room made her shiver after the cold of the outside as she slipped next to Abigail.

"There you are," her sister whispered. "Don't worry. Aunt Mildred didn't notice you were gone. She's too busy with Emily. Yet another man is completely smitten with our youngest sister."

Eliza smiled. As kind as she was lovely, it was easy for everyone to like Emily. "Don't be jealous. Is that baron still seeking you out regularly?"

Abigail rolled her eyes. "You know he is. He came to calling hours yesterday. Aunt Mildred says I should marry him but I'm just not..."

Eliza stopped listening. Because just behind Menace, she'd spotted another man. Tall and dark-haired, he stared back at her with a knowing smirk on his face. He was their mystery man from their carriage rescue. Here. Tonight.

His gaze held hers and he gave a single sideways nod of his head, gesturing toward the door to the hallway. Then he pushed off the wall and began to slowly make his way in the direction he'd indicated.

Her breath caught. Should she go? Should she tell Abigail?

But just then Baron Rumples arrived, requesting a dance even as Aunt Mildred, the major, and Emily continued to converse.

She let Abigail go, giving a smile of encouragement. This was what her sisters were supposed to do. Meet men they might marry. And she would continue to investigate their father's disappearance and their uncle's involvement.

Taking a deep breath, she started for the door.

The crowd was thick, and she lost sight of him several times but finally found him leaning against the door jamb leading out to the hallway.

Meeting with Menace had been one thing. Though he was a rake, she also knew he was her brother-in-law's dear friend. His relationship with Bash would keep him in check. Not only that but she inherently trusted him for some reason.

But this man...

There were no rules here.

She swallowed down a lump, her steps faltering. Should she continue to follow?

It was foolish.

But then again, she needed to make some progress toward a future for all of them.

Drawing in a fortifying gulp of air, she started for the door again.

CHAPTER THREE

CARMELLA'S HAND had slid from Dylan's elbow to his back and if he weren't mistaken was slowly making its way to his backside.

Had he avoided these parties? They were far more interesting than he'd ever imagined.

Not that he wished for Carmella's hand on his rump. In fact, he decidedly did not want her touching him anywhere.

Why didn't he just let the indebted title slide to the next heir? He could make enough to stave off the creditors and allow the rest of it to go to the devil.

And be the failure everyone assumed he would always be.

He frowned. What did he care?

They were right. He was a waste.

Carmella laughed, loudly, at her own joke and he joined in, not having heard a word. What did it matter?

He could propose tomorrow, and she'd likely say yes. It made him tired. This was going to be his life?

He sighed as Eliza passed by, her simple silk gown of cream shimmering in the candlelight. She was alone again and headed for the doorway, looking rather singular in her purpose. He pulled back his chin as he watched her. What was she up to?

He followed her gaze and then nearly cursed out loud.

Standing in the doorway, rakishly leaning against the jamb, was a man who was…well bloody hell if he wasn't just as tall, dark, and handsome as Dylan. And that man, whoever he was, was looking right at Eliza. Watching her progress across the room.

Dylan straightened, his back expanding as Eliza made her way through the crowd.

For a moment he wondered if he was mistaken.

She had some sort of pull over him. Perhaps he was imagining the entire thing. Surely, she wasn't attempting a second clandestine meeting within a half hour?

But as she drew closer to the fellow, he pushed off the wall.

And just like with Dylan, she stopped four feet away from the man.

Was he talking? It looked like he was conversing with her.

"My lord?" Carmella cut in. Her hand had come back up to the small of his back, but she was pulling on his coat, flapping it away from his skin, causing puffs of air to travel up his back. "Are you listening?"

He cleared his throat and looked down at the woman to whom he was supposed to pay attention. The one who had the potential to right his title and make him the hero of his family rather than the wastrel. "Of course, I am, my lady," he gave her a winning smile. "How could I not? Your story about…" He paused. What had she been talking about?

"My cat, Tulip," she huffed.

"Yes, of course. Fascinating." And then he placed a hand over hers, the one tucked in the crook of his arm.

She blushed. But it was nothing like Eliza's. Poor Carmella. Her skin turned blotchy with her spotted cheeks and neck.

Unable to help himself, he glanced up to see Eliza again, as he remembered the perfect pale hue of her cheeks.

But as he looked toward the door, he didn't see her.

He quickly scanned the room. She wasn't with her family. Wasn't crossing the ballroom. Where the bloody blue blazes had she gone?

"Anyway," Carmella cut into his thoughts again. "Tulip is the most perfectly behaved cat. Anyone who meets her declares her so. You should visit tomorrow for calling hours and see her. She's as beautiful as she is good."

"I see," he answered, barely listening. A jealous knot tied up his stomach. If that ass, whoever he was, touched Eliza the way Dylan had just touched her he'd...

"Will you?" Carmella leaned closer, her bosom brushing his arm. He resisted the urge to pull away. As if the difference in the two women needed such a definite comparison. And the truth was, Carmella didn't compare.

The problem for poor Carmella was a woman had just scrambled his mind with the same trick. "I'd be delighted," he answered, attempting to smile. "But if you'll excuse me, Lady Carmella, I've spotted an old friend. Until tomorrow?"

She beamed with triumph as he slipped his arm from her hand. He tried not to run as he made his way to the door. What if they'd slipped off to a room? What if that man was touching Eliza?

Then another thought made him stop dead in his tracks. What if the other man was hurting her?

He started again, sliding through partygoers as he sprinted toward the door. If he'd had any doubts about chasing after her, that last worry banished them. She might need him.

And perhaps, if she did, she might value him a bit more.

Bloody hell, when had he decided he wanted her approval?

But when he reached the doorway, all his thoughts vanished.

Because in the open, in the hall as people milled about, Eliza stood next to the tall, dark, and annoying stranger. They whispered with their heads bent toward each other. Well, mostly the other man whispered while Eliza listened. Unlike his meeting with her out on the terrace, she looked...comfortable. Her gaze was intent but free of any agenda. In fact, she barely spoke, just nodded occasionally as she listened to whatever he was saying her lips pursed in thought.

For a split second he began to turn around. This man was getting the real Eliza—the one she'd never share with him.

Why did that hurt? His stomach tightened and he clenched his fists.

But then...her gaze met his and she did the last thing he'd expected.

She waved him forward to join the conversation.

Eliza's thoughts hummed as her gaze met Menace's.

"You'll meet me tomorrow at dawn?" the other man whispered. John. That had been the only name he'd given her. "It's important."

She grimaced, her gaze drifting back to Menace again waving him over before she returned her attention back to John. He'd saved Emily's life two weeks ago. Which meant she gave him some measure of trust. But an illicit meeting in a park in the dark? Not even she was brave enough for that. "I can't."

He grimaced. "I have information I need to give you, but I can't risk being caught for both our sakes. I have to meet you away from prying eyes and ears in a place and time where we can be certain we're not followed."

"Caught by whom?" she asked, her voice dropping. "My uncle?"

He grimaced even as he tugged at his collar. "There are men far more dangerous than your uncle involved."

"Like whom?" Menace asked from just next to her.

"I can't explain here," the man whispered, glancing about. "I've taken a great risk even talking to Eliza tonight, but you should all know what's happening."

"And how does he plan to share information with you safely?" Menace asked, his hand coming to her back.

She looked up at him, feeling safer already with him at her side.

Strange. Just a few minutes ago, she'd thought Menace the danger.

"I wish to meet in a private location..." The other man stopped, staring down the hall. "Eliza will explain. I have to go."

And then he melted into the crowd, heading toward the grand stair.

Eliza watched him for as long as she could before she turned to look at Menace. Who was looking down at her with an unwavering gaze. "Who was that?"

"John," she answered, knowing the name didn't explain much. "He was the man who saved Emily a few weeks ago when our uncle attempted to abduct us from Bash's care. I recognized him. He's the very man I was asking you about on the terrace."

Menace grimaced. "That doesn't mean you should trust him."

She stepped closer to Menace. "He says that he knows where my father went and why he's been gone for so long. He also said he is my father's partner." Hope began to swell in her chest. "But he also wants to meet me just before dawn at—"

"Absolutely not," he returned.

"You didn't even hear where." She prickled. Not liking him telling her what to do. She'd enough of that with Bash and she could take care of herself.

"I don't care where. You can't go. Ladies don't meet men alone in the wee hours of the night."

She straightened away from him, irritation replacing the comfort she'd just felt. "*You* are giving lectures on how *I* should act?"

He tightened his grip on her waist. "I am." He frowned. "Even with me out on the terrace, you took far too many chances. What you are referring to as protection for your sisters, I say is reckless."

She tried to pull away, but he held her firm. "I'll have you know that this meeting is the only way to get any information. Information you didn't have."

"You don't need to get information at all. Most of the men who work at the club are researching on your behalf. They'll find out who he..." Menace pointed his finger up the stairs where John had disappeared, "...is and what happened to your father."

Eliza stiffened. "I don't want to rely on them. This is my chance—"

"No," he barked. "I appreciate that you are a strong, capable woman but there are lines you shouldn't cross."

Worry pricked along the back of her neck. How could he stop her? Then she bit her lip. Menace could tell Bash. That would be enough. Her brother-in-law would make sure she didn't go anywhere until this situation was solved. "You could come with me," she said, hoping he'd agree.

He grimaced. "Also no."

She put her hands on her waist. "You are insufferable, do you know that?"

"It's too bad you never met my mother. She'd completely agree," he said, with an edge to his voice that she'd never heard before.

She bit her bottom lip. "What if John knows where my father is right now?"

Menace paused. "If he did, why isn't John going after your father himself?"

"That's what I need to find out."

"What if I go?"

This time when he pulled her closer, she softened against him because...because he really did seem to have her best interests at heart. "I appreciate that, but you might not know the right questions to ask."

His frown deepened. "I hate to admit it but that's a valid point."

"See? We should go together. I can find out what he knows about my missing father and you can keep me safe."

"And if Bash discovers that we've had a rendezvous?"

That was a problem. She had plans and so did he and neither of them wished to be stuck with the other. She placed her hands on his forearms trying to think potential solutions through. "I'll lie and say it was some other man."

His eyebrows went up. "You'd be ruined. Are you on a mission?"

She shrugged. "I let go of the prospect of marriage and a happily-ever-after when my mother died. Even before that..." She looked away, not finishing that thought. "I'll make my own way."

He was quiet for so long she looked up at him, his face tight and tense. "Your own way?"

"Men aren't the only creatures capable of it."

"I'm sure they're not. And if you can do it, good for you. I don't seem able to." Then he stepped back. "I'll meet you at the kitchen door at four. Best not to sleep at all and change into something more serviceable."

CHAPTER FOUR

Dylan was a fool.

There was no other explanation. He should have stuck by his principles and not allowed Eliza to attend.

But she'd looked so…desperate and at the same time…determined.

And he knew she'd find a way. At least with him in attendance he could keep her safe.

Still, he should have told Bash and then perhaps he and Bash could go in her place.

He shook his head. She'd hate him if he did it.

But, then again, she'd be safe. And she'd stay far away from him. Which was how it should be. He had another woman to court. And as he stood there with Eliza, one thing had become clear. When he was with her, he couldn't seem to keep his hands to himself.

He sighed as Eliza hurried back to her family. He didn't bother to enter the ballroom again.

Instead, he made his way outside.

Once in his carriage, he didn't go home but rather he made his way to the Duke of Devonhall's home.

If Bash hadn't attended the party with his new bride that meant he was likely having a quiet evening at home. Dylan was sure to be interrupting.

Though matrimony had never been a goal of Dylan's, he had to confess that Bash seemed happier than he'd ever seen his friend.

He rolled his neck. Bash was sure to be bored stiff within a year.

Then again, the Carrington sisters had a way of keeping life interesting. Look at Dylan. Here he was in the middle of the night, about to bust in on a friend all because of Eliza.

When he arrived, he made his way to the front door and raised the knocker.

The butler opened the door immediately. Clearly, he was waiting for the sisters to return.

"I need to speak with His Grace. It's urgent."

The butler nodded and disappeared, but it took nearly a quarter hour for Bash to appear, and when he did the only word that might describe his normally impeccably groomed friend was…disheveled.

His hair looked as though someone had been running her fingers through it a great deal and his clothes had the rumpled look of having been in a pile on the floor.

Menace grinned despite himself. "Fun night?"

"It was until I was interrupted."

"Sorry." Menace grinned wider. "But Eliza is barreling toward trouble and I thought you should know."

"Eliza? Did you mean Miss Carrington?" Bash pushed out through gritted teeth.

"When discussing trouble, that would be rather nonspecific. There are several Miss Carringtons who currently reside here." Menace chuckled, not the least bit concerned over his friend's ire.

Bash snapped up straighter, combing his hands through his messy locks. "What kind of trouble?"

As quickly as he could, Menace explained about John's appearance and his request for a meeting.

Bash grimaced. "And she agreed, didn't she?"

"Worse." Menace cleared his throat. "She asked me to attend with her."

Bash's eyes narrowed. "When did you start speaking so intimately with my wife's sister?"

Menace held up his hands. "She approached me tonight. Frankly, I tried like hell to avoid her and, I swear, I am courting another woman."

"Who?" If anything, Bash looked even more incredulous.

"Lady Carmella Dumbly."

Bash's brows flew up. "Why?"

Dylan sighed. "You know why."

"You don't need her. She's damned annoying for one. But honestly…you'll get there on your own. Financially speaking. It just takes time."

Dylan shook his head. "You don't understand." Dylan had never stuck with anything in his life. He remembered his parents' disappointment when he'd failed out of Eton. He had to admit, he'd wanted to get kicked out. His parents never approved of anything he did. Why should he strive for their affection? Except, that had been the first in a string of failures that had become a self-fulfilling prophecy until he wondered if they were right. Perhaps he failed because he'd never been good enough. Not because he wanted to spite them. Now, he didn't trust himself to take the long way to financial success.

Bash gave him a long look. "I understand far better than you think. The club is digging you out of the hole. And you love it there. You'll stick with it. We'll make certain that you do. That's what the rest of us are there for. We'll help you."

Menace looked down at the plush carpet under his feet. Nothing like his own rundown townhouse. Grim determination steeled his spine. He'd make it great again. "I appreciate your confidence."

"It's fact." Bash said. "Now go upstairs and get a few hours of sleep. You and I will be attending that meeting."

"And Eliza?" Menace raised his head again. A bit of regret tickling down his spine. She wanted to do this. She would be furious in general and with him, specifically. He imagined she was formidable when angry and likely glorious.

"She stays here. Even with both of us there…" Bash shook his head.

"Isabella has hinted at some of the things Eliza has done to keep them safe. She needs to stop taking risks."

Menace raised a brow. "I'm not sure that's who she is."

"Well, regardless. She can't come with us to this meeting. It's just too risky."

Menace shook his head. He'd have to tell her himself what he'd done. If she was going to be angry, she might as well find out from him.

Eliza had changed out of her formal entire and into a riding habit. The sky was still black. But she and John had agreed to meet before the first rays of sun so that she'd have time to return undetected.

His words had sent chills down her spine.

Her uncle was just a small part of a group stealing from her father. No wonder the thefts had remained undetected for so long. But that still didn't explain why her father hadn't returned.

Her heart ached in her chest.

In her heart, she'd felt abandoned by her father. He'd left her for months at a time to help her mother throughout her childhood. And then, Eliza had had to care for her while she was ill, and finally, prop up her sisters when they were all alone.

His lack of care hurt, but it also made her angry.

What if she'd been hurt, or ruined, or…?

But she hadn't. She'd been able to carry the burden, and for that, she was grateful.

But if he could come back now, she'd be free.

Able to start on the life that would just be hers.

She thought of Menace and the way it felt when he wrapped his arm about her waist. Her eyes fluttered closed.

In those moments she nearly forgot that she wanted to go off on adventures. Whenever he was near, it was as though the adventure had come to her.

At that moment she heard the doorknob to her room rattle.

She looked over, and sure enough the metal moved. Holding up her candle, she slid closer.

Once again, the knob jiggled and, not knowing what else to do, Eliza grabbed onto it, stopping its movement.

"Eliza?"

Menace. She'd recognize the deep timber of his voice anywhere. "We're supposed to meet by the kitchen door."

"I know that," he answered.

"Then what are you doing here?"

The knob jiggled one final time and then stopped. "That's a bit complicated."

She frowned. "Complicated? What's complicated about the kitchen?"

He let out a sigh. "Eliza."

There was a warning in the way his voice dropped low. Something that let her know he'd changed his mind. She needed to think fast. "We'd better hurry. If Bash catches you in the house, there'll be no escaping."

"He already knows I'm in the house."

She blinked in confusion. "What?"

"I arrived here before you did."

Why would he come here before her? A gasp escaped her lips. "What did you do?"

She heard him press against the door. "First, I told Bash of your plan."

"You did what?" Then his words sunk in. "First?" What else had he done? Her heart raced in her chest. She shouldn't have trusted him. Drat. She slapped her forehead, frustrated.

"I know you're a risk-taker. It's honestly something I greatly admire. You're determined, and focused, and intelligent. But you're also in danger."

She smacked her hand on the door. This needed to be done. Her missing the meeting would only delay their ability to put all of this behind them. All because of Menace. "You don't get to decide if I go or I stay."

"Bash does," he answered. "Which leads me to the second thing I've done."

She'd had just about enough of this conversation. She yanked on the door, but it didn't budge. Not even a little. She gasped, yanking harder.

"I barred the door," he said quietly. "It's for the best."

"Who's best?" she shot back pulling one more time. She knew the door wouldn't budge but she needed to vent her frustration somehow. He needed to open the door so that Eliza could attend this meeting. He didn't realize how important that was, although he clearly understood how determined she could be.

"Well," he paused, and she heard him press closer to the door.

She pressed closer too. Because if by some miracle the door opened, she wanted to be close enough to hit him. "Well what?"

"Certainly mine. If you hate me then I won't have to worry about how distracting you are."

"Cad," she fired back. "How can you be so selfish?" Hate him? Hate didn't even begin to describe how she felt about him right now. She'd like to beat him senseless. Anger pumped in her veins. But something else beat along with it. Excitement? Challenge? She pushed those thoughts aside.

"But it's for your best interest too, Eliza."

She wouldn't be able to hit him. He refused to open the door, that much was clear. And so, she'd have to cajole. "Menace," she started her voice dropping into her best impression of a purr.

"Dylan," he replied. "Early-morning conversations require a certain level of intimacy."

"Dylan." The name felt good on her tongue. "Listen. Stop trying to protect my reputation. I'm not going to marry."

"What?"

"That's right. I might become an actress. I'd be good at it."

"I've every confidence."

"Have you travelled outside of England? What is the rest of the world like?"

He cleared his throat. "Eliza. I need to ask you something."

"What?" She cocked her head to the side.

"Has someone compromised you?" She heard the knob rattle again.

"Let me out and I'll tell you."

He chuckled then. "Do you need me to kill him? Because I will."

That made her soften and some of her anger melted away. "No one compromised me, Dylan. I am still…" Her cheeks heated. How did she tell him she'd done more with him tonight than any man ever? "I just don't want to marry."

"Why not? I thought all women wished to marry?"

"Not me." She took a step back from the door. "My mother spent half her life waiting for my father. I've been waiting for him for the past year. What kind of life is that?"

"Oh," he said.

"How comforting." She took another step back because as she looked to her right, she realized something very important. Her room had a connecting door. "You'd better be going. You don't want to miss John."

"John? The man couldn't give you a last name?"

"Nope. Secret identity and all that."

"Eliza?" His voice had dropped low again. "What are you doing?"

But she didn't bother to answer as she slipped through the other door.

CHAPTER FIVE

Dylan rubbed his forehead as he stared at the door. Why had she gone silent?

"Eliza?"

He scrubbed his hand down his face. He supposed it was better. He needed to go, and he could spend all night…what…talking?

Christ. He was worse than Bash. At least his friend was lucky enough to have married the lady he desired and was spending his time rolling about the bed… Then he paused. Had he just used the words married and lucky in the same thought?

He was going mad.

But striding down the hall he made his way through the kitchen and out to the barn where the carriage already waited.

The door was open, and Bash sat inside. "What took you so long?"

"Locking a lady in her room takes a bit of finesse." Dylan snapped the door shut and took the seat opposite his friend.

Bash let out a grunt of dissent. "You did what?"

The carriage began moving, heading toward Hyde Park.

"How else were you going to keep her from coming?"

Bash sat forward giving Dylan a dark glare. "I planned to calmly and rationally tell her, when she arrived at the carriage, to go back inside. That I could handle it."

"You obviously don't know Eliza very well."

Bash pointed right in Dylan's face. "And you are far too familiar. One wrong move and you won't be marrying Carmella Dumbly."

Menace shrugged. "That's your threat? Oh my saints. Not marry Carmella? How will I survive?"

Bash let out a low rumble. "But you'll marry. Don't play dumb with me. You know very well what I mean."

Dylan sat forward in his seat ignoring Bash's finger. Which was jabbing in his direction. "Tell me. What's being married like?"

Bash dropped the finger. "I hesitate to answer."

"Why?"

"Because." Bash ran a hand through his hair. "What you are proposing with Carmella is the exact opposite of what I chose with Isabella."

"And what did you choose?" He pressed his hands together in front of his face as his elbows came to his knees.

Bash looked up at the ceiling, seeming to collect his thoughts.

"When I met Isabella..." He paused again. "I felt this instant need to keep her safe. And when we're together, I can barely breathe. She fills me with so much..." He stopped. "I've never experienced anything like it, and I doubt I will again. It's the best thing that's ever happened to me."

Dylan swallowed. He viewed marriage as something to be endured. Certainly that was how it had been with his parents.

Would he grow to be protective of his wife in time?

Then he thought of Eliza and nearly choked.

He was protective of her already. More so than he'd been with any other person in his entire life. "Are you certain you want to keep Isabella safe because you love her? Perhaps she just really needs you."

Bash smiled. "Maybe. But then again. I didn't fall in love with any of the other sisters. Just her. Obviously."

Bash had him there.

He felt no great need to keep Emily or Abigail out of trouble. Although, they didn't have the same penchant for it.

The carriage began to slow, and Bash peeked out the window. Just on the edge of the park stood a lone horseman.

"The first thing I want is a last name. I'm not calling him John. I don't care if he makes one up."

Bash laughed at that. "I'm not even certain I know your given name."

"Good," he grunted. But it made him think of Eliza again. The way his name had sounded on her lips. What would it sound like after a passionate kiss?

Bash snapped open the door, yanking him from his musings. "Let's get this over with." And then his friend climbed out.

He followed.

As they stepped down, the sky was lightening the smallest bit. To his right he caught a flash of green and looked to see Eliza jump down from the footman's seat. "What the devil?"

She gave him a winning grin. "You're going to have to do better than that if you want to keep me from what I'm after."

Bash actually chuckled next to him. "Bested by a woman."

"What is funny? She's at a clandestine meeting at dawn."

"It's not clandestine. I'm her family. And he's…" He waved toward the lone rider. "A man who saved her life once already." And then Bash glared at Eliza. "And you should have stayed home."

She ignored Bash entirely and looked at Dylan. "He stuffed me rather unceremoniously into that very carriage." She pointed back. "I told you I wasn't missing this."

Then she lifted her hand as though she expected him to offer his elbow. Which he did. As her hand slid against the sleeve of his coat, he leaned close to her ear and whispered so that Bash could not hear, "I swear that if I ever get you alone, I'm going to spank—"

WHY DID the idea of him lifting her skirts and touching her behind fill her with…wicked longing?

She ached and throbbed deep inside. She should be furious with him. He'd attempted to lock her in her room… To keep her safe.

He'd learn that it was a useless endeavor.

Then again, he likely wouldn't. He was off to woo another woman while she…she was off to do whatever she wished.

But she didn't want to think about the future now. First, she had to find out what John knew.

They approached the man on horseback who climbed down from his saddle. "This isn't the sort of meeting I'd had in mind."

Bash stood taller. "This is the only one you're going to get." His lips thinned over his teeth, stepping in front of his sister-in-law. "*We* have to keep Eliza's safety in mind."

The other man stepped forward. "You're implying I didn't consider her safety. I assure you, I did. A lover's tryst, at least that's what it would have looked like, doesn't arouse much suspicion among thieves and criminals. But a summit…" He grimaced as he waved to the four of them.

Bash grunted in acknowledgement, but Dylan was not ready to give the man any ground. "We'll get to the danger in a moment," Dylan bit out. "Let's start with a name. Yours."

"It's better that you don't—"

"He's Menace," Eliza answered. "A name of his own creation. And he goes by Decadence," Eliza pointed at Bash. "When he doesn't want others to know who he is."

The other man gave a quick nod. "In that case, call me…Dishonor."

"I don't like it," Menace returned, pulling her a touch closer.

"Stop," she softly replied before turning back to Dishonor. "How long have you been my father's partner?"

"Three years," he answered. "After he caught your uncle skimming from the books, he decided he needed help. Someone he could trust to help run the business."

"And how did he know he could trust you?" She asked, glad to be holding Dylan's arm. His muscles flexed under her fingers.

"I'm the son of an old friend."

"All right." She inhaled a deep breath. "So what happened then?"

"Just as I joined the company, your father tightened up the books. He began going through all the ledgers and what he found scared him."

Eliza wanted to ask what and why, but she waited for him to continue instead.

"On the surface, they appeared perfect. But when he crossed them with actual deposits, he found large sums of money were missing. Had been for a while. What was more, they continued to be missing after your uncle was cut out of the business."

"Oh," Eliza breathed. "Was someone else stealing from father besides Uncle Malcolm?"

He shook his head. "I think initially these people were skimming off the profits with Malcolm's help. As far as I can tell, Malcolm owed them money, and this was his way of repaying them. And in case you're wondering, he still owes them. Part of his behavior now is out of desperation and not just cruelty."

"He's trying to sell me into marriage," she snapped back then checked herself. She wasn't angry with this man. "Sorry," she murmured. But she felt Dylan draw her closer again.

"Don't apologize. I wanted to help you from the first. I'm sorry I've left you alone. I've been watching though, to make sure you didn't get into too much trouble. There were a few times I nearly interceded."

She swallowed as Dylan let out a soft groan. "She's got a penchant for trouble."

That was beside the point. "Who are these men and where is my father?"

"Your father…" Dishonor drew in a long breath. "As near as I can tell, is gone."

"Gone?" she whispered, her throat closing. Something in the way he said it implied he wasn't just missing but…

"His secretary returned a few months back to report that…" Dishonor hesitated, "to report that your father has passed on. He was killed, I'm afraid."

Eliza's breath stalled in her chest and she clutched Dylan's arm. In her heart, she'd hoped he'd return. And she realized something else. She'd missed him. She'd been so busy being angry, she'd forgotten how much she cared. Sadness rose up, making her chest ache. "But he's supposed to come back and take care of my sisters and—" She couldn't keep going before her voice broke.

Dishonor shook his head. "I'm sorry. I had to tell you because I knew you'd be strong enough to hear it..." He paused when Dylan let out another deep growl of disagreement. "It turns out your father isn't the only man this group is stealing from. He did travel to the Orient but not to secure a new contract. He was investigating; though, for my protection, he didn't give me all the details of what he'd discovered to send him that far away."

"Who?" Bash asked. "Who else are they stealing from?"

Dishonor pinched the bridge of his nose. "The Crown."

"Bloody fucking bullocks," Dylan ground out.

"The only reason I'm still alive is because the crime ring responsible doesn't know who I really am. And the only reason the girls have been left alone is because they don't know anything."

"Didn't," Dylan added. "They didn't know anything."

"Hence the secrecy." Dishonor pointed around the garden. "But there is good news."

"What?" All three of them asked at once. She'd been fighting back tears but now...

"Your uncle had your father declared dead, remember?"

"Of course," she answered. How could she forget?

"Well, I own ten percent of Carrington Shipping. Each of you now holds twenty. We're partners."

"Shut the..." Dylan started but Bash hit his arm.

"You're one of the richest women in England."

"Oh." Eliza's finger tightened on Dylan's arm. She was likely leaving marks her fingers were digging so tightly into his flesh. She had the money to do as she wished. Why didn't that make her happy?

"Is this good news?" Bash asked. "Doesn't that put them in jeopardy? If they're part of the business, will these criminals try to hurt them? Should I hire guards?"

"As long as everyone assumes they are in the dark about the theft, they should be fine." He cleared his throat. "I'd cease trying to wed your sisters for now. I'm worried some of the suitors might actually be part of the crime ring responsible and pose more danger than they'd do good."

"Oh," she said again. Where had her words gone? Eliza considered herself able to handle most anything. Perhaps it was the night without sleep, but this turn of events was making her head swim and her eyes burn from unshed tears.

"Eliza?" Dylan's voice was achingly gentle as he slipped his arm about her waist. Her knees grew weak and though the sky was getting brighter, darkness descended over her eyes. She fought the weakness, but she was afraid she might faint.

CHAPTER SIX

Eliza's knees buckled and Dylan pulled her tight against his side, both arms wrapping about her middle. "When was the last time you ate anything?" he asked close to her ear.

She pressed a hand to her cheek, disoriented. "I don't know."

She didn't know a lot of things. How was she going to keep her sisters safe if they didn't marry?

How would she ever leave England, her uncle, and the repulsive Mr. Taber behind if her sisters were still in danger? The simple answer was she couldn't. They were hers to protect and always had been. But she wasn't likely to leave England anytime soon. And how was she going to tell her sisters that their father was gone forever?

Hanging onto his memory had been the one light that had pulled them through the darkness of their mother's death.

Her head swam and Dylan pulled her tighter against his chest. She heard him speak but didn't really process the words. "Is there anything else we should know?"

"Keep her safe," Dishonor answered. "I know where the club is. I can get information to both of you there."

She rested her head on Dylan's chest and she was aware of him half-carrying her back to the carriage. If Bash was concerned about the familiarity, he said little as he followed behind them.

He was right. She was tired. Deep down in her soul, exhausted.

He didn't even bother to try and hand her into the vehicle. Instead, he swung her into his arms and climbed in, settling her on his lap. She was like a limp rag. She couldn't seem to get her body to work no matter how hard she tried.

Bash cleared his throat. "Menace."

"Not now," Dylan grit out, settling her even closer.

She didn't resist. He was strong and warm as he supported her full weight, cradled against his large body.

She wrapped her arm about his waist and that's when she realized that she was crying. Big tears that slid down her cheeks and landed on his waistcoat.

And then a sob broke free.

He didn't know this, of course, but she'd hardly even cried when her mother had passed. She'd allowed herself a few private tears when her sisters couldn't see, but she'd had to be strong for them.

But held against Dylan, she couldn't push back the wave of emotion that crashed over her and another sob broke loose. It was as if she was finally able to grieve. Here, in this moment, she didn't need to be strong. He could hold that job. She was free to allow her feelings out.

He held her tighter to his chest, his cheek coming down to rest on the top of her head. "I've got you," he said in a whisper. "And I'm not going anywhere."

She swallowed down a lump as she continued to cry.

He stroked his hand up and down her back, his deep voice low and melodious as he mumbled unintelligible words of comfort.

How had she not realized what a relief it would be to rely on someone else? She'd needed her sister, Isabella, of course. But she'd never given over control like this.

She didn't wish to be weak, but it was so…nice to have someone else be her strength for once. And somehow, she trusted him to still respect her, to support without judgment. The magnitude of that thought settled over her. Never in her life had she given over this sort of control to another person. She trusted him…

"I…" she started, her voice breaking on the single word. "I don't know why I'm so upset. I just…"

She shook her head, rubbing her face along his coat. She was lost in this moment. Where did she go from here?

"You learned your father is dead, and your plans needed to be put on hold, and that your uncle is even worse than you thought. Allow yourself a good cry, love. You've earned it." The words were murmured into her hair and they sparked a fresh round of tears. And another wave of appreciation.

"I'm never leaving England, am I?" she asked into the quiet of the carriage.

She felt his smile against the top of her head. "That is up to you still. Didn't you hear the man? You're rich."

She drew in a sharp breath. It seemed to fill her lungs with air but her muscles with some strength. "Are you suggesting I leave my sisters to fend for themselves?"

"First off, I don't think you should go anywhere," Bash said from the other seat.

Eliza started. She'd forgotten Bash was there. But of course he was. He was her guardian now; he wouldn't have left her in a carriage alone with an unmarried man.

She'd gotten used to being independent in those months they'd been without either of their parents.

A plan was beginning to form in the back of her mind. Hazy and unclear, she needed some solitude to put it all together.

Which she'd get later. Right now, she intended to stay in Dylan's arms. Because as much as she valued her independence, there was something undeniably wonderful about relying on this man's strength.

"Try to understand, Bash," she murmured, not bothering to turn her head and look at him. Dylan's chest made the perfect pillow and her eyes fluttered closed. "I want to travel, see the world, do exciting things. I wasn't meant to just embroider or sit at tea."

Dylan chuckled and it reverberated through her cheek in the most pleasant way. She tilted her head back to look up at him. "Amen to that."

"You don't want to sit idle either?"

He shook his head. "I've never been good at it. I like change. Excitement. It gets me into trouble a fair amount."

She nodded as her hand fluttered to his chest. She could feel the strong beat of his heart underneath her fingers. "I understand completely."

Bash cleared his throat, loudly and obviously. "Eliza, are you ready to sit on your own?"

"No," Dylan answered before she had to. "She's fine right here."

She turned deeper into his chest. She was fine. Right here. Despite one of the worst mornings of her life, she was completely fine wrapped in the strength of his arms.

She'd have to leave soon enough, and she'd need to figure out her future. She shuddered to think about it, and he held her tighter to his chest.

She burrowed in. Despite what she'd just said about adventure and freedom, she had the feeling that she belonged here, wrapped in his strong embrace.

Dylan squeezed her tighter.

He'd known needy women before. Hell, he'd known nearly every type of woman. But there was something about a very strong one curled into him that pulled on every heartstring he had.

She normally faced the world with her shoulders straight and her head held high. It made him feel strong to think that she, of all people, needed him. His family certainly didn't value him, but Eliza did and that meant something. Didn't it?

And in this regard, he wouldn't let her down. He'd comfort her until he couldn't anymore.

The depth of his conviction frightened him a bit. He couldn't remember feeling this strongly about anything.

Once the carriage pulled up to the house, he'd send her inside and go home.

He'd allowed her too much sway over him tonight.

Dylan didn't become involved in other people's lives. He could barely manage his own. And marrying a woman like Carmella would finally prove that he was the son his family had always wished he could be. He'd do the right thing. Not that they were alive to see it, but still.

He remembered the countless times he'd let his family down.

He'd arrived at a cousin's wedding completely intoxicated. He'd heard about that one for days.

Granted it was Henry's nuptials, who at the time had been heir, and the man his parents constantly held up as the shining example of proper behavior in contrast with Dylan's own personal failings. But still. Dylan was the one who'd made an ass of himself in front of the entire family. He supposed embarrassing them was his way of getting back at them for never being enough.

And then there was the affair with Henry's wife he'd had later on. The poor girl had been starved for affection. But that's not why he'd done it. He'd somehow wanted to prove that one person found him more desirable than dear Henry.

He closed his eyes as shame washed over him.

Eliza's hand tightened around him.

But the memories, they pulled him away from her. He wasn't worth the ground she walked on. She was spectacular. Beautiful, strong, the pillar of her family, and he...he was a destroyer. He'd worked his utmost to spite the family that never cared for him. Never wanted him.

That's all he'd ever done.

With his marriage, he was attempting to build up one thing...the title. But he knew he'd personally let down whatever woman he married. How could he possibly be a success at both when he'd never done a thing right in his life?

"Dylan?" She lifted her head.

"We're nearly there. You should eat and then go straight to bed." He gave her a soft smile, trying to disguise his inner turmoil.

"Thank you," she said, her voice hoarse from the crying. "I don't know how I would have…"

He ran his knuckles down her cheek. "You would have found a way."

She gave him a breathtaking smile. Her mouth started to turn up, hesitated, and then gently lifted into a warm, soft grin that robbed the air from his lungs.

He'd wanted her before but somehow this was different. He still wished to touch her, but he also wanted…to protect her, support her. Watch her shine.

"Thank you," she murmured as the carriage slowed to a stop.

He didn't answer as the door snapped open. Then he lifted her out and when his feet were on the ground, he gently set her down, placing a hand at her waist to guide her up the stairs.

The trio made their way into the still-empty kitchen where Eliza grabbed a hunk of bread from the counter and then started up the stairs.

She didn't say a word, but she looked back at him several times until she disappeared from sight.

He stared at the point where she'd disappeared for several seconds before a hard finger tapped his shoulder. "We need to talk."

Bash.

His best friend in the world. And the man who currently participated in wedded bliss. Damn. What had he been thinking holding Eliza in front of Bash like that? Eliza had a way of making him act unlike himself. "Do we?"

"I don't know about you, but I could use a whisky." And then Bash started out of the kitchen. Dylan followed.

When they reached Bash's office, he wordlessly crossed the room and opened the decanter that sat on a small table, filling two glasses.

Dylan stood by the low fire, watching the embers burn in the grate. Bash handed him a glass and he took a sip, enjoying the sweet burn as they sat.

Silence settled for a few minutes as they both drank.

Then Bash rubbed his forehead with his thumb and finger, his head tilting down. "That was so awful."

Dylan looked over at him. "It was." He remembered the way Eliza had curled into him.

Bash lifted his head again, his face stony. "A ring of thieves stealing from the Crown? Endangering all of the sisters? I thought I was protecting them from one angry uncle. But this…"

Dylan winced. That was an excellent point. Why didn't he think of these things? He hadn't considered beyond Eliza being in danger. "Are you going to listen to him? Keep the girls out of society?"

Bash shook his head again. "I don't even know. On the one hand, we should keep up appearances. They're safe because no one knows we know anything. If we suddenly change our behavior…"

"It's like the sisters know about their father and the danger." *Damn.* Bash had a point. He ran his hand through his hair. How were they going to keep them safe? When had he counted himself in this?

Then he snorted into his whisky. The moment he'd agreed to go to a dawn meeting with an unwed woman, he'd firmly placed himself amidst the drama.

"I need you to help me, Menace," Bash said, closing his eyes.

His friend looked tired. "How?" He gripped his glass tighter.

Bash rolled his glass between his hands. "Well." His hands stilled as he turned to look at Dylan. "You could marry Eliza. That would help."

He choked on the whisky sliding down his throat and just managed to push out the word, "How?" once again as he attempted to keep the drink from spraying out of his mouth.

Bash glared. "For starters I'd have another well-titled lord aiding me in keeping them safe. As Carrington Shipping gets rolled into our assets, it becomes less appealing to other men to steal from us."

"Not true. If Dishonor is correct, they are stealing from the Crown. If they'll take from the Prince Regent…"

"Then we have a powerful ally."

"You're using the word *we*," Dylan bit out. "You're a duke. You don't need me."

"Let me say it a different way. Eliza is now an heiress. Not only would you be helping your friend, but you'd get what you wanted as well. I've seen the way you look at her. The way you just held her. You had to know there would be consequences for such familiarity."

He grimaced. A woman as smart and savvy as Eliza would hate the way he drained her to finance his needs. She'd hate *him* at the end of it. Hell, his own parents didn't even like him. When they'd been alive. "And what about what Eliza wants? You heard her. She doesn't want to be tied down by marriage."

"All the more reason to marry you."

"How do you figure?" He took another large drink. The long night made the alcohol go straight to his head and he rubbed the heel of his hand along his forehead.

"You'll give her protection now and freedom later. Together, we'll insulate her sisters. Quietly find them matches that can be trusted with the business as we help Dishonor identify this ring. And by the way…" Bash leaned forward. "Carrington Shipping isn't like a dowry that brings in a one-time payment. You'll make money, year over year. It's better than any other potential bride price."

A wave of understanding made him sit back in his chair. Bloody hell, Bash was right.

He pushed his fingers into his eyes. "I need to talk with Eliza. She should know…everything."

"Smart choice." Bash reached over and clasped him on the back. "See? You're perfect for her."

He shook his head.

He'd seen disdain in his mother's eyes until the day she'd died whenever she looked at him. It would kill him to see the same emotion reflected in Eliza's.

He was the furthest thing from perfect he could be.

CHAPTER SEVEN

Eliza slipped into her room, too tired to even undress.

"Here. Let me help you," Isabella said as she rose from Eliza's bed.

"What are you doing here?" Eliza asked, grateful to see her sister.

Isabella winked. "You taught me this trick, remember? I knew you'd be tired so I warmed your bed for you."

Eliza sighed with relief. "Thank goodness."

Isabella worked off Eliza's clothing one piece at a time. "Did you learn anything?"

"More than I wanted to know," Eliza whispered. How did she tell her sister that her father was dead?

Isabella stopped and wrapped her arms about Eliza. "Father's gone forever, isn't he?"

"I think so," Eliza answered, her voice trembling.

"Do you know how?" Isabella whispered, squeezing Eliza tight.

"I forgot to ask, but I know his secretary witnessed the event." Eliza shivered.

"He wasn't the most present father. I know you loved him but…"

"I did. But now, I realize just how much he left us alone and how much was foisted on you. We almost gave up our very lives for the sake of the business."

Eliza thought she'd cried all the tears but her eyes misted again. Because her sister actually understood. "Thank you."

"You're welcome." Isabella gave a heartfelt sigh. "At least it's over and we know the truth."

"Isabella," Eliza said, the warning ringing in her voice. "It's so far from over that it isn't—" She couldn't continue, not now. Sitting down, she pulled off her boots and slid into the bed. She was only half undressed, but she didn't even care. "I'll explain everything after I've had some sleep. I'm so tired."

Isabella slid into the bed next to her sister, wrapping her arms about her. "I understand. Get some rest. You can tell me everything when you wake."

Eliza let out a long sigh. "Can I tell you a secret?"

"Undoubtedly."

"I don't want to marry." Eliza let out a long, jaw splitting yawn.

Her sister held her tighter. "And what will you do instead?"

"Be an adventurer."

Isabella's breath blew into the back of Eliza's hair. "Then I shall miss you terribly while you're gone. I always knew you were the strength of this family. So like father."

Was she leaving her family like he'd done? "I'm not like him," Eliza fired back. "I'm here when my family needs me. I've always been here. He left me to do his work years ago."

Isabella squeezed her sister harder. "I meant that you have his spirit. And you're right. We've been so lucky to have you to protect us. You deserve whatever future you dream of and I'll support you no matter what."

Her shoulders sagged. Why didn't those words sit well with Eliza?

She wanted to go away, didn't she?

But as her sister pressed close, she thought for the first time about how much she'd miss her family. How much family meant to her. Had always meant. What if they needed her while she was gone? What if they didn't?

They'd have husbands. Children.

And she'd miss them, she realized. She'd been so focused on breaking free she hadn't considered what she'd lose.

"Isabella." She looked back at her sister. "Your kindness is as deep as your strength."

"So is yours." Then her sister slipped from the bed. "I've gotten it all warm for you. It's time for you to sleep. When you wake, you'll tell me everything, won't you?"

"Absolutely," she answered, closing her eyes. She couldn't keep them open another second. "Thanks for being patient."

Isabella chuckled. "Look at you. How could I not?"

Then Eliza pried her eyes open and lifted her head. "If I tell you, will you share with Emily and Abigail? I don't think…" She wasn't sure she had the strength today to tell her sisters they couldn't court, something they'd been enjoying a great deal, and that they'd lost their father.

Isabella gave her a tight nod. "Whatever you need."

Eliza shook her head before laying back down on her pillow.

In the past few months, Isabella had become Eliza's rock.

Her sister's loving presence had filled Eliza in her weaker moments. Like now. "Thank you." Then she lifted up, pushing her hands down in the mattress. "I love you."

Isabella stopped and then turned back, crossing the room and tossing her arms around Eliza. "I love you too." She held her sister tight. "No matter what you just learned, you know we're going to get through this together. Right?"

Silly tears sprang to her eyes again.

Perhaps Eliza wasn't as strong as she'd always believed. She certainly wasn't now. But that's what family was for. Would this have all been different if her father had believed in their bond? If he'd confided in them? Stayed and faced things together?

She eased back from Isabella. "You are the best sister a woman could ask for."

"The feeling's mutual." Isabella gave her one last squeeze. "Go to sleep. We'll talk in a few hours."

Eliza nodded and slid down into the bed. Sleep overtook her before the door had even closed.

Dylan woke trying to figure out where the hell he was. He sat up and looked around, scrubbing his eyes.

Then he remembered.

After a few drinks, Bash had invited him to sleep in a guest room rather than travel home.

But as he climbed from the bed, it occurred to him that Eliza was here. Under this roof. Likely sleeping too.

What did she look like when she was in bed? A vision of her brown hair spread across his pillow with her arms opened and relaxed, welcoming him, filled his thoughts and he scrubbed his face. He should have gone home.

Because a few hours of sleep had cleared his mind and left him...wanting.

He wanted Eliza.

He'd stripped off his clothing and sat with his bare feet on the floor, cradling his head while he went through all the reasons why he shouldn't take her. It would be selfish. But then a voice argued, he'd be helping her too.

He'd never done anything good in his life.

But then a new thought occurred to him. If he thought marrying Carmella was a good idea and Eliza a bad one, perhaps he should marry Eliza after all. Do the opposite of what he thought was the correct choice. Surely there was logic in that. At least with his record of poor decision-making.

He rose, then began to wash and then dress, grimacing at his clothes from the night before. They'd have to do.

He made his way to breakfast, hoping to find the room empty.

He was still trying to decipher his feelings, Bash's words, and Eliza's wishes.

But as he approached the room, he heard people talking. Females. Soft worried voices, cutting into him like the tip of the blade.

"Father's truly gone?"

"No more courting?"

"Running a business? We're not suited to that." Then a pause. "Well, perhaps Eliza is."

"I'm not." Eliza. Her voice held its usual strength. Louder, a mezzo soprano that was more sultry and confident than any of her sisters. But underneath that…was it just him or did he hear a new brittleness in the tone? "But Bash is. Unfortunately for him, he's got a rather lot to worry about."

Isabella chimed in. "If this man…Dishonor, had been running the business, surely he can continue. Do we need to do anything?"

Silence fell.

Finally someone cleared her throat. "What do you think, Eliza? Do we need to do anything?"

"Yes. Something. But I don't know what yet. I've met this man twice and he kept his identity secret from us for months. I'll not trust him with our entire future. Not yet."

"It's not Isabella's whole future and it won't be ours once we marry. I say we keep courting."

He shook his head. He was eavesdropping. Pulling his coat straighter, he stepped into the doorway. "Excuse me, ladies."

They all turned toward him, plates of uneaten food sitting in front of each of them.

"My lord." Eliza rose and then gave a quick curtsy. "Please join us."

"I don't mean to interrupt," he said, not moving into the room. "His Grace and I ended up talking until the sun was well into the sky and it seemed easier to stay than to travel home."

"Oh no, you're not interrupting at all." Isabella waved him forward. She'd once posed as a man and dealt cards in his gaming hell so they knew each other quite well, and her easy smile made him more comfortable now. "Come eat. It will be a good reminder for us to eat as well."

Dylan gave a stiff nod. "I don't mean to insert myself. But His

Grace and I were discussing your very topic last night. What Dishonor said was that he was worried some of your potential suitors might be part of the crime ring. They'd hope to marry you so that they might gain ownership of the business, making it easier to continue to pilfer from the books."

One sister gasped while another gave a cry. "Do we cease socializing?"

He grimaced. Should he not have shared that? "Unfortunately, to disappear from society might cause more suspicion."

A very lovely woman he thought might be Emily nodded her head. "Oh, that does make sense."

Another huffed. "So we're just going to keep traipsing about the streets of London like sacrificial lambs?" He looked at the fourth sister. Was it Abigail?

He ran his hand through his hair. "Isabella…" he cleared his throat. "Would you mind chaperoning a meeting between Eliza and myself?"

"Of course," Isabella answered at the same time Eliza let out a huff of breath.

"I don't need my little sister as a chaperone."

He quirked a brow. Somehow, he relaxed with her irritation. This was Eliza. And this was why eldest sisters usually married first. Having a younger sister chaperone would chafe most women.

"It's for your protection," Isabella started. "Society—"

"I don't give a fig about society." Eliza sat back down and determinedly stuck her fork in her plate of food. "Eat, my lord. And then we will go in the sitting room next door and we'll be certain to leave the door open in case society arrives."

He couldn't quite keep from chuckling as he crossed to the buffet. A man might as well have a full stomach before he proposed a sham marriage.

CHAPTER EIGHT

A HALF HOUR later Eliza sat across from Dylan, the silence stretching out between them. The door was open, and she was absolutely sure her sisters were all pressed to the wall just outside the room listening to every word.

She drew in a deep breath as she blinked to keep from rolling her eyes to the ceiling. An audience didn't make this awkward at all.

"Do you know where I am supposed to be right now?" Dylan asked, stretching out in his chair, his long legs crossed at the ankles in front of him. He looked large and masculine and…delectable.

"Where?"

"I am supposed to be meeting Carmella's cat." He gave her a lopsided grin as he chuckled out loud.

Her stomach twisted at the boyish gesture. He looked even more handsome like this, relaxed and happy and virile. "I beg your pardon?"

"Carmella. She wished for me to meet her cat." He swiped a hand down one cheek. "That is what I could be doing right now. Courting a woman and her feline."

"And instead here you sit with me." She straightened in her chair. "Where will you find a new heiress?"

One of his brows lifted. "Hmmm. Let me think. Heiress? Heiress? Where might I meet one of those?"

Her mouth dropped open. Because she should have known that was where this conversation headed but somehow…she hadn't. "But I've already told you. I don't wish to marry."

From the hall, she heard the faintest gasp. Standing, she glared at the open door.

"I am well aware, which is why I have a proposition for you." He stood too, moving closer. "But first, I need to tell you about me. I want you to know the truth about me, what you're getting into, before you decide."

A warm sensation slid down her chest. He trusted her, she heard it in those words. "All right. Just give me one moment." Then she crossed over to the doorway, peeked out, stared at all three of her sisters, who had the decency to look embarrassed, and then shut the door, turning the lock. "Pray, continue."

He pressed his mouth together, suppressing a grin, as she came back over to him.

"Eliza." He reached for her hand, slipping his fingers into hers. "I've done very little right in my life."

His hands were large and warm, his skin sliding along hers. "How so?"

He shrugged. "The typical mostly. I drink too much, carouse too often. My family was very serious and I never seemed to belong."

She winced. "That must have been difficult."

"I suppose it was, but I didn't help matters. I went out of my way to be even more troublesome…"

"Not surprising. You're a strong man. If you'd just fallen in line, you'd be weak. I'm not much for doing what others tell me to do either," she said, then gestured back at the now closed door.

A look of surprise crossed his face. "I'd never thought of it that way. Likely because I mostly destroyed opportunities and relationships with my behavior." His face hardened as a dark shadow crossed his face. "While you strengthen the people closest to you."

She reached out and touched his sleeve. This was the man who'd carried her into the carriage this morning when she'd fallen apart. "That's not what I see."

He looked into the fire. "You don't know me very well. But I want you to understand this before you accept or deny my offer. I've disappointed everyone who has ever cared about me."

Her throat thickened as she listened to the pain in his voice. She didn't see the man he described. He was a marquess. A successful club owner. Her personal hero. "All right. I understand."

He leaned onto the mantel staring into the fire. "I need a dowry to help me bolster my title."

Her fingers curled into her palm but she didn't say anything as she allowed him to continue.

"You need to protect your sisters and solve this mystery so that you might go on your adventures."

She started in surprise. Adventuring was part of this deal? "And?"

"I propose we join forces."

"Join forces?" She stepped closer to him, raising her brows.

He reached out and hooked her waist, pulling her close to his body. "Marriage, love. We get married to help each other accomplish our goals."

She looked up at him. "Just so I'm clear on this. As your wife, I will just sail off to America and leave you here?"

He shrugged. "That's what I was thinking."

She shook her head. "And you'll run my share of Carrington Shipping?"

He shook his head. "We'll have to hire someone. I mentioned already that I'm not the best with responsibility."

She slid her hands up his arms, then linked them behind his neck. "And the club? How do you run that?"

He looked down at her. "That's different. My friends fill in my gaps."

She rose up on tiptoes. "And do you think you and I might be able to…fill in each other's gaps?"

"What gaps do you have?" He shook his head. "Near as I can tell, you're perfect."

"I can assure you." She glanced toward the door again. "If you brought my sisters in here, they'd have a completely different opinion." Which was the truth. "I'm hardheaded, uncompromising, demanding, to name a few." She threaded her fingers into his hair. And he had done what she'd never expected from any man, he'd offered her freedom within the confines of marriage. The man who already felt like an adventure even when they only travelled as far as the library.

He chuckled as he bent lower. "Take as much time as you need to consider my offer. But as your husband, I'll do my best to help Bash and your family."

Her mouth opened and closed again. What did she say? The idea had merit. How much, she didn't know. She did know that his very presence made her mind murky and heavy. Could she make a good decision here in his arms?

But before she could answer, his lips descended down on hers. Firm but warm, his mouth moved over hers, causing a cascade of tingles all through her body.

―――

ELIZA FELT DIVINE. Her lips were soft and sensual, her body fitted against his perfectly.

Why had he kissed her?

This wasn't supposed to be part of the plan. They were to lead separate lives.

She'd been so tempting against him, he'd dipped his head down and stolen this kiss.

And now…

Now he couldn't stop.

She tugged at the strands of his hair, pulling him closer as he slanted her mouth open and brushed his tongue against hers.

He felt her tremble, her heartbeat quickening against his. It was like adding lamp oil to a fire. He pressed her closer, the curve of her hips, filling his hands.

Their kiss deepened and lengthened, their tongues sliding against each other over and over as they ground together. He wanted this woman.

Had from the first.

And now that she was in his arms, he didn't know if he could stop.

But he had to.

His body refused to cooperate. A problem he was well acquainted with. He never followed the path he should.

That thought made him rip his mouth from hers.

Eliza, her body still pressed to his, gazed at him with hazy, passion-filled eyes, her cheeks flushed, her mouth puffy.

Dylan nearly came undone. It took every ounce of control not to dip his head back down and take her lips again.

Drawing in a cleansing gulp of air, he squeezed the roundness of her hips. "We can't."

Her chin pulled back. "Can't? Why not? Didn't you just propose?"

His eyes drifted closed as he continued to hold her. Pulling himself up straighter, he attempted to remember all the reasons that he'd wanted to keep distance between them. "Yes. I proposed. An arrangement. A business partnership of sorts. One that does not involve such personal connections."

She sucked in a breath stepping back. "Your club is based on personal connections."

He grimaced as he resisted the urge to pull her closer again. "Not like this."

Her arms wrapped about her chest. "So you want to marry but not be intimate?"

"Something like that." He supposed he hadn't fully considered the implications of Eliza moving into his home for some length of time while he kept a respectable distance. As usual he was mucking up this plan.

She dropped her arms, her shoulders pulling straighter. "Forgive me but both our futures rest on this decision. I think it's time that we decide upon a few more details."

Scrubbing his face, Dylan twisted his neck, a crack filling the air.

What had he gotten into this time? "How can you venture off to America if you've had a child?"

She blinked then. "That is a valid point." Eliza turned away so that he looked at her profile as her chin dropped. "I don't see myself as the sort of woman who would abstain from a physical relationship nor would I ever abandon a child. For both those reasons, I think it best that I say no to your offer."

"No?"

"No." Then she started for the door. Without another word, she opened the heavy wood panel and left the room. Left him standing and staring where she'd disappeared.

CHAPTER NINE

Eliza reached the hall and leaned against the wall, covering her face. What had she just done?

Unfortunately, she'd forgotten that all three of her sisters were also there…waiting. They descended like a flock of vultures.

"What happened?" Isabella asked.

"Did he hurt you?" Abigail demanded.

Emily touched her arm. "Should I get Bash?"

"No and no," she said as she pushed back off the wall and started down the hall. The flock followed. "And I don't want to talk about it."

Abigail huffed behind her. "Sorry but that isn't an option. What happened that has you so upset?"

She stopped, spinning around to her sisters. "He proposed."

All three of them stopped too and she was met with three blank stares.

"You're upset because he proposed?" Emily asked.

"Yes," she fired back then turned and began walking again. "It wasn't a real proposal and even if it was, I don't want to marry."

"There was so much in that sentence, I hardly know where to begin." Isabella lifted her skirts and took a few running steps to reach Eliza's side. "Oh wait. I do know. Why wasn't it a real proposal?"

"He asked me for a sham marriage. One where I kept my independence and he kept his hands to himself. Well, except for my money. That he'd touch in spades," she said, unable to keep the bitterness from her voice.

Emily gasped behind her. "Oh, dear."

Eliza had a moment to wonder if she were just offended that he'd rebuffed her but then she held her head higher. That wasn't it. She had a plan. And it didn't involve a delinquent marquess.

Of course, it also hadn't involved a ring of thieves.

Isabella reached for her shoulder and gave it a light squeeze. "For heaven's sake, Eliza. Stop."

Eliza did. But she spun about again. "Why?"

"Because," Isabella gave her sister a long look. "There's a lot of parts to this and we need to work them all out."

She twisted her hands into her skirts. "Must we?"

"I'm afraid so," Abigail answered.

"Fine." She pointed down the hall. "Let's have a seat in the library."

With a nod, the group made their way to the vast room, settling in a cluster of chairs. Eliza didn't wait for them to ask any more questions. With a deep breath, she detailed his proposal.

When she was done, Emily slid her fingers into Eliza's. "Now tell us why you don't wish to marry."

Eliza shook her head. That was...harder. "I know you loved mother and father. And I know their relationship was miles better than either of our aunts' but..." She drew in a deep breath.

Isabella leaned forward. "It's all right. You can say it."

Eliza touched her chest, willing the fear away. "Father was gone so much. And mother needed help. And I..."

"You took on the burden," Abigail answered.

She nodded. A burden she'd have to pass on to potential children. "It's not that. I love all of you. And I love our relationship. But I don't want to be left behind by a husband to wait and to worry. I..." Drat. She wanted a real partnership. One where they did things together. Made choices together. Adventured, or stayed home, or had children...together.

With startling clarity, she realized what her actual goals in life involved. It wasn't that she needed her independence as much as equality. She wanted a partner.

Which, he'd offered.

But she also wanted...her hands flew to her mouth. A wave of heat spread across her. She wanted him.

A soft groan escaped her lips. "I turned him down."

"We know that part," Isabella replied as she scooted closer. "But explain why."

"I want a man who wants me too, but also respects that I am capable and not meant to just be a pretty bauble on his arm. I—"

"Forgive me for saying so." Emily squeezed her hand tighter. "But he outlined a whole plan with you. One where he tried to give you what you wanted. Perhaps rather than denying his wishes, you should have opened negotiations. Unless you just don't like him?"

No. She liked him. Far more than she should. "Deep down I think I might be afraid he doesn't want me. Not nearly as much as I want him."

"Eliza." Isabella smiled softly. "Men always want you. And once you are intimate...I have a feeling he'll be completely entranced."

She shook her head. "I allowed my temper to get the better of me. Didn't I?"

"Perhaps," Emily said. "But that's only because you care. Talk to him again. But decide what you want first. Do you truly want to venture off to America alone? Because we own a shipping company now. You can go whenever you wish. But perhaps you and your husband could go together. Learn the business. Build up his title and our business. Together."

Eliza looked about at her sisters. She'd taken on a great deal of responsibility but not alone. They had been behind her from the first. Guiding and helping. It was Isabella who had lifted them out of poverty and landed them here.

Did Dylan have a family like this? From what she'd heard, the answer was definitely no. They'd torn him down rather than building him up.

What he needed was a family like hers. People that would support him. Help him see the clear path when his mind was clouded. Just like she had with her sisters. How many mistakes might she have made without the three of them? And Dylan needed to understand that. It was support he was lacking not judgment.

And what did she need? She'd always thought she wanted her independence but today... Today she'd come to a different answer...

The question was: Had she ruined her one chance with Dylan?

DYLAN SAT ON A FLUFFY, pink chair as a long-haired white cat hissed at his feet.

He hated being here, hated that he had to do this.

Now that he thought about it, Eliza was not perfect. In fact, she was damned annoying. He'd helped her with her mystery, but his bride search? She'd turned him down and offered only Carmella as a possible candidate. She wasn't holding up her end of the bargain.

He swiped at the back of his neck. He should march right back to the Duke of Devonhall's and demand she give him more names and then he'd kiss her senseless. His teeth clenched. He'd been the one to end that kiss. Not her.

The damned cat took a swipe at his boot, leaving a long scratch mark in the dark leather.

That was going to take forever to buff out.

"Isn't she just a doll?" Carmella gushed from a matching pink chair as she reached down and picked up the offensive animal.

"A doll," he replied dryly, his eyes casting up at the ceiling. Perhaps this hadn't been the best choice.

He'd been so irritated with Eliza and her swift departure that he'd left Bash's house, went home, changed, and then travelled straight to Carmella's. Where he was now ensconced in pink décor that was accented by white cat hair.

Carmella lifted the fluffball up to her face and buried her nose in the animal's fur. The thing hissed again, but Carmella ignored the sound, giggling as she cooed words of love into the cat's hair.

Dylan blinked as he attempted to picture this future. His house bathed in pink as cats swirled about his feet.

And his wife barely paying attention to him as she heaped affection on her pets.

He'd rather have his spouse off in America.

He let out a sigh of frustration. His gut clenched. He'd rather have Eliza.

Carmella was...not for him.

But Eliza had rejected him, and he wasn't here because he'd ever had an affection for Carmella. He was here to save his marquisate.

It was just...that he thought he might rather sink into a hole than live this life.

His parents had never given him credit for a single thing done right. Even when he'd saved a farmer's horse, they'd chastised him for getting dirty. A marquess's son must always be ready to present a pristine and cultured façade. Who cared about a filthy animal?

This was his chance to prove he was more valuable than any of them.

And yet...

He sat straighter. Could he do it without a Carmella?

He'd been slowly digging himself out of debt. But some of his creditors were growing restless.

Would one of his friends give him a loan? The very idea filled him with shame.

Men married dowries when they needed money. It didn't feel honorable but then again...it was the way the peers dealt with these sorts of problems. A division of assets. He brought the title, she brought the money.

But even referring to it as assets made him think of Eliza and the business proposition he'd suggested. Not like the beautiful, vibrant, intelligent woman she was.

"I'm desperate to find a male cat as wonderful as Tulip. I shall name him Buttercup and—"

"Buttercup?"

She gave him a sly smile. "Unless you'd prefer I called you, Buttercup?"

"No, I don't think—"

"It has a ring to it, as a pet name." Carmella set the cat down and leaned closer to him. Her hooked nose came within inches of his. "What do you say, Buttercup? Shall we get cats and make kittens?" She gave him a long sly glance, her lips curling into a thin-lipped smile.

The innuendo was not lost on Dylan and he had to applaud her veiled reference. In another situation he would have found it amusing.

"I'm more of a stallion than a buttercup." He leaned back, putting distance between them. First this was a lesson on how a man wanted to be treated, talked to. Second, he was not interested in participating in Carmella's game. "How do you feel about horse flesh?"

He was an avid rider. There was nothing he liked better than to ride breakneck through the park at dawn. But he already knew Carmella wasn't the sort. Not that it mattered, really. Most men didn't marry women who shared their interests. Still, he had the feeling Eliza would be an excellent horsewoman. And she most certainly was not planning a cat breeding program.

"Horse flesh?" She wrinkled her nose. "What's cuddly about that?"

He suppressed a grin. He couldn't tell her that what he really craved was the sort of tup that was short on cuddling. He wanted a wild ride and he knew where he'd find it.

Hell, Eliza had rejected him because, in her own words, she wasn't interested in abstinence. That's what he was pouting about? He ought to be celebrating.

But he needed a wife.

An answer to his financial problems.

And he got the impression that if he didn't keep Eliza at an emotional distance, he'd lose his head entirely. Which always got him in trouble.

Tulip swiped at his boot again. "I suppose nothing, but then again, I'm not certain what's cuddly about that?" And he gave Tulip a nudge with his offended boot.

The cat hissed and Carmella cried out. Quickly, she picked up the hissing cat and began stroking the beast's back. "Don't worry, Tulip. I won't let the mean man anywhere near you again."

Dylan rose. He'd managed to mangle a second courtship today, but he didn't feel nearly as sorry about this one.

Without saying goodbye, he headed for the door. He wasn't sorry to end his short relationship with Carmella, but Eliza was another situation entirely.

That, he needed to think on.

And this time he needed to come to her with a much more developed plan.

CHAPTER TEN

THE NEXT EVENING, Eliza stood on the outskirts of the Applegates' ballroom, surveying the crowd.

By all accounts, she and her family shouldn't be here. However, they'd decided it was less suspicious if they continued to socialize. They'd declined half their invitations but had decided to attend the other half, mostly smaller venues.

But this party they'd already agreed to, so here they were in a throng of dancers.

Dylan had attended with them. Even now, he stood several paces away, talking with Bash and Isabella.

She'd wanted to talk to him too, but she wasn't certain what to say. *I'm sorry I declined. Would you ask again? Can we clarify several points?*

None of the words seemed quite right and so she'd said nothing at all and neither had he. Still, he was here and that counted for something. Whether out of allegiance to her or Bash she wasn't certain, but before the night was over, she'd find a way to talk with him.

Eliza had watched all evening for anyone suspicious. Not that she'd been successful.

The men all looked like the usual suspects. Well dressed, slightly bleary in the eye.

She had seen neither her uncle nor Mr. Taber, which was a relief.

Her toe tapped but not to the music. Instead, it was a rhythm in her own head. How was she going to solve this mystery and discover who was endangering her family?

She huffed a breath as she pushed away from the wall. Mr. Taber was part of the crime ring and his interest in her had been clearly stated. Perhaps she should allow him to court her after all.

But the very idea made her shiver in revulsion.

Swiveling her head, she saw her sister, Abigail, with Aunt Mildred while Emily danced with the major they'd met a few nights ago. Eliza's eyes narrowed. Was he one of the thieves?

Then another figure caught her notice out of the corner of her eye. Mr. Taber.

His normally hunched shoulders were drawn down even lower as he talked with another man that Eliza didn't know.

Then the two, still deep in conversation, began making their way out to the terrace.

Eliza watched them for a moment, unsure of what to do. Their conversation could be about nothing. Then again, they could be discussing the very topic on which she was searching for answers.

Without another thought, she started after the two men. She slipped out of the ballroom, just in time to see the two men start down a path. Here in the quiet night a few words filtered toward her ears. "I've found the warehouse. Cheapside."

More whispers she couldn't hear.

"Fennington Street."

She slipped down the path, following them. They left the terrace and started down a tree-lined path, bushes closing off the lights and noise of the party. She could hear better but could hardly see. "He knows about us. He's shut down several of our lines. But if we can get the goods at the source, from his warehouses, it doesn't matter how many lines he eliminates."

"We could drive him out of business. Then what?"

"He's driving us out of business. And we need to deliver. Our lives depend on it. If we have to, we'll kill him too."

"But the sisters. They own most of the company. Malcolm, the fool, saw to that."

"He'll pay too. That's already been arranged."

How would Uncle Malcolm pay? But she'd forgotten all about him as the two men stopped and Eliza stopped too. Had they heard her?

For a few seconds, she stayed motionless, afraid to breathe. She hadn't seen them for some time, she could only hear them.

And now, she was in the deep, dark part of the garden where no one could see her either.

Then Mr. Taber spoke again. "And the sisters are easily dealt with. Plans are already in place."

She breathed a sigh of relief. If they were still talking, they didn't know she was there. Then his words penetrated, and she stood straighter. Plan. What plan?

Suddenly, a hand reached out and clamped over her mouth. Before she could even scream, she was being dragged against a large man.

This was not Dylan. She'd know the feel of him anywhere.

First, this man smelled disgusting and while his arms were hard bands of steel, his middle was…squishy.

She pushed, trying to wriggle away but he held her firm.

"Well," Mr. Taber cackled. "If my little doe didn't step right into the middle of the hunt."

She pushed all the harder, trying to bite at his hand but he held firm, nearly suffocating her his arms were so tight. "You've eluded me for far too long, Eliza. But now you're mine."

Sick dread filled her stomach as she attempted to get her hands between them to push at his chest. But he started dragging her deeper into the garden and suddenly her back slammed into the thick trunk of a tree, bark scraping her bare shoulders.

She cried out but he only laughed louder, the sound both excited and triumphant. Her stomach rolled and vomit threatened to rise from her gut.

He used his body to press her tighter to the trunk as he dragged up her skirts. She tried to push his hands back down but she could barely breathe and then…

Just like that, a loud thud filled her ears and Mr. Taber was gone. He slid to the ground in a heap, her eyes following his descent as she continued to lean against the tree for support. She could barely catch her breath as she stared.

"Eliza."

Her name snapped her out of the trance, and she looked up to see Dylan in front of her.

She threw herself at him, nearly tripping over Mr. Taber but Dylan's strong arms lifted her up and with a speed she thought impossible, especially in the dark, he carried her back down the path. But he didn't take her inside. Instead, they went through the garden gate and out into the alley where a line of carriages waited.

"What are we doing?"

"You can't go back into the party, love," he whispered in her ear, still carrying her.

"I can't?" She blinked, looking up at him.

He stopped for a minute and gently pulled a twig from her hair. "I don't even want to know what your back looks like."

She gasped in a surprised breath. He was right. She must look frightful. And she was so grateful he held her in his arms, once again providing a strength she desperately needed.

Finding his carriage, he yanked open the door as he called to the driver. "Find the Duke of Devonhall and bring him here. Quickly." He slid into the carriage, still holding her against his front. Sitting on the bench, he settled her on his lap. "Are you all right?"

She nodded, burying her head into his shoulder. "I am now." Then she curled into him. "I have tried to tell you that I am independent and able to take care of myself, but you keep proving me wrong."

He gave a small chuckle, wrapping his arms tighter about her. "I saw you leave. I wasn't actually attempting to follow you. I just wished to talk."

She nodded against his front. "I don't care in this moment if you were following me. I'm just glad you came."

He kissed the top of her head. "Me too."

She lifted her head. "Besides. I'm beginning to realize I was never as independent as I believed. My sisters. They bolster me regularly."

His eyebrows rose at that. "I find that admission...surprising."

"That I said it or that I think it?"

"Both," he answered.

She shrugged. "Then prepare yourself to be amazed. I've got a great deal more to say."

Dylan looked down at her, his chest tight. He wanted to hold her. Kiss her in comfort. Hell, he couldn't wait to hear what she had to say. "I await your words with bated breath."

She smiled then, slipping her arms about his waist. "May I ask you a question first?"

"Yes."

"Did you ever once feel supported by your family? Did they validate any of your decisions?"

That made him tense. "No."

She shook her head. "No wonder."

"No wonder what?"

"You don't trust yourself." She tipped her head back further. "How could you when no one ever trusted you."

He stared down at her, snapping his mouth closed when he realized it was ajar. "They didn't trust me because I am no good."

"Not true," she softly whispered. "Do you think I am no good?"

"You are the best," he answered fiercely.

She gave him a glowing smile. "Thank you. I just made a terrible error in judgment following Mr. Taber. It's only because of you that I am safe and unharmed."

He tightened his grip on her, shame filled him. "You don't know some of the choices I've made."

"You can tell me sometime. If you want. I'll tell you some of mine too. One time I convinced a baron to strip naked and then stole his clothes."

"What?" He sat straighter, worry and a bit of irritation coursed through him. "You did what?"

"I didn't take off any of my clothes," she answered softly. "Just took his and ran."

He shook his head. "Eliza—"

"I know. Foolish. Reckless. Addlebrained. At least that's a few of the choice words my sisters used. The point is...I'd make some terrible decisions without them. And let's be honest, increasingly without you."

Something deep inside him softened. "But if neither of us makes good choices then..."

She shrugged. "Maybe. Or perhaps we'll know we have to watch out for the other person. Be a team and—"

The carriage door wrenched open.

"Bloody fu—" Bash stopped, glaring at them. "Tell me what's going on this instant." Then Bash climbed in and took the seat across from them, sitting with a heavy thud.

Dylan remained silent, allowing Eliza to explain what had happened in the garden. As he held her, he contemplated her words. A team?

The idea had merit.

He needed a system of checks and balances and so did she, apparently.

But he forgot about his thoughts as she started to detail what she'd overheard. "They said that *he* was on to them and that they knew where his warehouse was and that *he* might need to be eliminated."

"He who?" Bash asked.

She shook her head. "They didn't say but they did mention Fennington Street and I know my father bought property there. We went with him to look at it as an overfill warehouse for his business..."

Bash sat back in his seat as he scrubbed his face. "I went to see the solicitor earlier today. I have full access to the records and the addresses. There was no Fennington Street. I'm sure of it." He leaned forward then, his arms resting on his knees. "What's more, Dishonor is right. The books look perfect, but the totals don't add up. The vendors sign off on goods received and money counted but then their actual sums are short. A large shop in Chesterfield and another in Dover have regular shortages."

Dylan furrowed his brow. "Can't we follow those shipments and see what happens?"

"Or have one of us infiltrate the company and try to aid in the shipments to those stores? But my guess is those runs have regular men who work them and are always on them."

"Then those men must work for the thieves and not for Dishonor."

"Yes. Let's start by following them. See where they go and who they talk to here in the city."

"But what about Dishonor?" Eliza asked. "What if he's the *he* they are referring to?"

Bash winced. "He's a man who can take care of himself."

"No." Eliza slid off Dylan's lap, sitting up straighter. "He currently runs our profitable business. He saved our lives not once but twice."

Dylan raised his brows. He could feel the tide rising in Eliza and he had a feeling these were the moments when she made her less-than-stellar decisions. It was a chance for them to test their system of checks and balances. "Bash and I will find the warehouse and warn him."

"I'm coming," she said, her fists balling.

"No," both men answered at that same time. Dylan knew she wished to be part of the action, but this was dangerous. If all she'd said was true, there could be an attack on this warehouse.

"You're not." Bash added. "I let your surprise trip to the park go but—"

"You let it go?" Eliza said, her voice growing louder. "You let it go? I've let your bossiness go. Which is not easy, either." She threw up her hands. "Dukes."

"Eliza," Dylan said, touching her arm. They still had a great deal to discuss but this wasn't the time. "We'll go to the warehouse. You've had enough excitement for one night. Besides, someone needs to stay with your sisters."

She pulled up even taller. "I thought you understood. I don't want to sit at home and wait. That's why I didn't wish to marry. I was never meant for that life."

Silence met her words. Because Dylan didn't understand. But in this, he didn't want her there. It might be dangerous.

"I can fire a pistol, you know." She crossed her arms. "I could dress like a man like Isabella did. I could—"

"You could be hurt," he replied sliding a hand down her arm. "If I die, the next dullard cousin gets the title. If you die…your sisters…"

Her shoulders hunched and she looked at the floor. "I understand. You're right. But—"

He shook his head. He wanted her safe. But she wanted…adventure. Action. Even after what had happened tonight, she wasn't afraid. "We'll go during the noon hour tomorrow."

"What?" Bash barked.

Dylan shook his head. He was going to regret this. Another bad decision to add to the list of personal failures.

But either he met her goals or his. And today, he chose her…

CHAPTER ELEVEN

Eliza shifted, attempting to adjust to the feel of men's trousers. They were…odd. Isabella had worn pants like this every day for a month and Eliza had thought nothing of it. But now, with them on, she was aware that every curve from the waist down was on complete display. And Dylan was aware of them too. His eyes had been on her rear since he'd picked her up this morning.

Dylan had kept his word and they sat outside the warehouse, carefully tucked in a doorway as they waited for someone to leave or arrive.

But he'd kept his hands to himself.

He didn't have a choice really because Bash had insisted on coming too. And the duke had grumbled about the ridiculousness of the decision ever since they'd left. Eliza didn't care. Let Bash lament her being here. Dylan had understood. And that mattered.

But Bash kept at it and finally tired of hearing him, Eliza had sighed. "You didn't grouch this much when I snuck on the back of the carriage and attended the meeting with Dishonor."

He gave her a level stare in return. He sat across from her, his knees pulled up to his chin, while Dylan was next to her in the same position. The narrow doorway wasn't meant for three people, especially not ones as large as the two men.

Bash growled in the back of his throat. "We knew who we were meeting then. And we were in Hyde Park. This is different." He leaned closer. "We could stumble across anyone. Friend or foe."

Eliza grimaced. He had a point. But so did she. "I'm able to do this, Bash. And what's more, I never intend to be a normal lady, so don't bother trying to shove me into that role. The moment my parents were both gone, and I had to take care of my sisters, any hope of me being that woman disappeared."

Bash clamped his mouth shut, not answering as he stared at her. But something softened too. "It's not that I don't understand how strong you had to be to keep your sisters fed for so many months, it's just that…"

"I like me better like this, Bash." Then she reached out and patted her brother-in-law's hand. "I'm learning that I don't have to do it all alone." She glanced over at Dylan. "But I don't want to go back to waiting in the drawing room for the man I care about to return. I'll never do that again."

Bash's eyes lit with understanding and Eliza was so grateful.

Just then, the sound of footsteps echoed off the stone, and whatever Bash might have replied was lost. All three of them looked out at the large double doors of the only warehouse on Fennington Street. They were carefully padlocked closed.

The steps grew louder until finally two men came into view. But to Eliza's relief, it was Dishonor himself who stood in front of the massive doors. The other man to his right. Eliza narrowed her gaze. The other gentleman looked oddly familiar.

As if Bash had the same thought at the same moment, he said, "I've seen him before. The one with Dishonor."

Dishonor's companion was tall, broad, his vest made out of a Scottish tartan. He whispered low to Dishonor, but Eliza couldn't make out the words.

"What should we do?" Dylan asked. "Once they're inside, we've lost our chance."

"Let's do this, then." Bash stood. "You two stay here."

Eliza made to protest but Dylan placed his hand on her arm.

The instant Bash stepped out of the shadows, both Dishonor and the other man turned.

Bash held up both his hands. "I've come with a warning."

The Scot turned and left, without a word, Eliza craning her neck to see where he went.

"Where is your friend going?" Bash asked.

Dishonor shrugged. "He's not ready to meet you."

"Why not?" Bash stopped, his hand dropping to his hip.

Dishonor shook his head, something dark and unreadable flashing in his eyes. "I didn't want to reveal myself either. Secrecy is key to safety."

"That's what I came to talk with you about." Bash started moving again. "Last night, Eliza overheard Mr. Taber and another man talking."

Dishonor's eyes widened and Eliza shifted. She wanted to be out there too.

"Come inside," Dishonor said, inserting a key into the lock. Eliza heard it click. "We'll talk more there."

Eliza tugged on Dylan's shirt. "Should we?"

"No," he answered, lacing his fingers through hers. "As Isabella's husband, Bash is a partner. He has every right to be here."

"I have every right to be here," she fired back.

But Dylan only smiled. "We'll watch out from here."

She knew what that meant. They'd allow her to come but they were going to keep her hidden in the shadows. Out of any danger.

She sighed. Men.

She supposed she should be more worried. After last night, she knew caution was important. But she'd also moved them far closer to solving their mystery. "I've been relegated to lookout."

"As have I," he answered with a smile. "It's an important job."

Her brow lifted. "Two lookouts?"

He gave her a wink. "Well, I'm looking out for you. Which in those trousers, is a damn fine job. I'm rather enjoying it."

That made her smile too. "Want to hear something naughty?"

His gaze darkened as he leaned closer. "From you? Always."

That made her insides tingle in the nicest way. "Not that kind of naughty. Abigail actually suggested that I stuff a stocking down the front of the..."

But his gaze had grown even darker and he made a low guttural groan that seemed to echo through her body. "Eliza, you are torturing me."

She wanted to ask him how so, but he leaned down until his lips were only a breath away from hers. "And we've yet to finish our conversation last night. About being good for one another."

She swallowed, letting out a little sigh as she stared at his mouth. "We do need to finish that. Yes."

He slid his hands down her neck, the light touch of his fingertips causing her to gasp for breath.

She wanted to kiss him. She wanted to tell him she'd made a mistake rejecting his offer but once again, footsteps echoed down Fennington Street.

DYLAN WANTED this woman with every fiber of his being.

His fingers itched to slide down the trousers and see if there were stockings stuffed in the front. Then, he'd like to explore further...deeper...

He stopped his imaginings as he heard the footsteps. Silently, he pressed Eliza further into the shadows of the doorway as three men came into view.

Eliza gasped and he knew why. One of them was Mr. Taber.

"You see the man next to Mr. Taber? He was with him at the ball last night."

Several choice curse words rose to Dylan's lips. Eliza shouldn't be here.

"Lock's missing." The third man pointed. "Means they're inside. Now is our chance."

Eliza and Dylan watched in silence as the three men slipped into the shadows.

He scrubbed his face. Bash would come out of those doors straight into a trap. But then again, the moment he left this doorway, they'd know he was there, and Eliza would be vulnerable.

His fist clenched against his thigh. This was the exact reason he didn't want to bring her.

She shifted and a small firearm appeared from inside her jacket. "Do we attack now or wait?"

He looked back at her, his brows lifting, despite the gravity of the situation. She never ceased to amaze him. "I'd prefer not to do a surprise outnumbered attack with you as my second," he whispered. "Then again, they could hurt either Dishonor or Bash before we've acted."

She grimaced. "I see the problem."

They sat silently for several seconds both attempting to come up with a solution when a cat crossed in front of the doorway. Noticing Dylan, the kitty veered inward, rubbing her side along his leg.

Eliza reached out and snatched the cat into her arms, rubbing along the cat's back.

Dylan was amazed the animal didn't protest but she curled into Eliza's arms.

"You're petting a cat now? Of all times?" he gritted out a whisper between his teeth. Women.

"Shhhh," Eliza said, giving him a small wink. "This kitty is going to help us."

"How?" he whispered back.

"Watch," she said as the door lock on the inside began to rattle. Bash and Dishonor were going to come out any second.

"I can't get away from women and cats," he muttered, but he had to be honest, his fingertips tingled at the idea she had a plan.

He should have known...

Eliza unfolded herself, standing with the cat in her arms. The alley door to the warehouse was some six feet away and he knew the three men stood in the deepening shadows just beyond.

"Be sure of foot, kitty, and run like the wind as soon as you land. I'll come back for you once this business is done." Then she looked at him. "Be ready to rush them."

His eyebrows rose. Sure of foot? What was she going to do?

He tensed, his muscles getting ready to spring when the door swung open and Dishonor stepped out. At the exact moment that the first man broke from the shadows, lunging at Dishonor. In that second, Eliza tossed the cat directly at Dishonor's chest. The cat hissed and clawed as it sailed through the air even as Dylan lunged from the shadow of the door. Dishonor caught the animal automatically, but the other man paused for that critical moment, and Dylan nearly roared with satisfaction as he tackled the man to the ground.

Mr. Taber and the other man jumped into the fray, but Dylan couldn't attend either of them as the man he'd tackled spun and rolled, getting Dylan underneath him and planting a good punch right into his gut. Distantly he hoped Dishonor and Bash had been ready and Eliza stayed hidden.

Dylan let out a groan as another punch hit his midsection but then, getting his hand free, he clipped the man with an uppercut to the jaw. The assailant fell like a sack right on top of him making the air rush out of his lungs before he pushed the other man off.

Bash had Mr. Taber pressed up against the wall while Dishonor, bleeding from several scratches, had knocked the third man to the ground.

"Tie them up," Dishonor said as he wiped some blood from his cheek. "It's the Bow Street Runners for them."

"No," Mr. Taber gasped from his spot on the wall. "You might as well kill me right now."

"That could be arranged," Dylan said, standing. Rage coursed through him as he looked at the man who'd attacked Eliza the night before. He'd like to mangle the man's face, but he remembered that Eliza would see it all and he forced himself to breathe. Dishonor stepped inside and then came out again with balls of twine. Tossing Dylan one, they began to tie the two unconscious men and then stepped toward Bash and Mr. Taber.

The man began to fight harder and Bash gave him a quick punch to the stomach. "If you're going to die anyway, you might as well tell us who you work for."

Mr. Taber sneered. "I'd never betray him."

"Is it he who is going to kill you?"

Mr. Taber laughed as Bash and Dishonor tied his hands. Dylan watched Taber, looking for any subtle cues. "It is. But if I talk now it will be a slow death instead of a quick one. And if you're smart, you'll allow him to keep pilfering from your business. He won't run it dry and you'll be safe. But get in his way and you'll end up exactly like your partner."

Eliza gasped from the shadows and then stepped out. Dylan didn't hesitate. He pulled her into his embrace, turning her away from Mr. Taber.

"Well look who it is." Mr. Taber leered. "My bride-to-be."

"*My* bride-to-be," Dylan snapped back.

Eliza tilted her head up and gave him a smile. It was gentle and warm and full of...whatever it was, it stole his breath.

"You can't have her. My associate has already decided that as the oldest, she should marry within our operation. Even her uncle has agreed. You might have moved the sister in with you, but he is still their next of kin."

Bash pushed the man into the wall. "He is not. When he left them in that house all alone, he forfeited his rights. I've already had a judge sign them over to me. You'll never touch any of the sisters."

Dylan squeezed Eliza tighter. Who was Mr. Taber's boss and how dangerous was this man that he thought he had rights over a duke? How would Dylan protect Eliza from this mysterious man?

CHAPTER TWELVE

Darkness had fallen by the time they could make the trip back to Bash's home. Dishonor rode with them and the cat slept soundly in Eliza's lap.

The soft purring helped calm her nerves and she stroked the animal, grateful it was unharmed.

The little ball of fur had been completely fine, but Dishonor was a slightly different story. "That thing scratched the hell out of me." He touched one of the cuts crisscrossing his face.

"That thing saved your life, I'd wager," Dylan replied.

"True," Dishonor said as he touched his cheek again. "What will you do with the animal now?"

"Keep it," she answered, giving it another pet. "It's clearly an alley cat. It'll enjoy Bash's barn and it'll be far better fed there." Then she looked at Dylan, her face heating. "And my marquess over there has an affection for women with cats."

Dishonor scrunched his brow… "Is that some sort of sexual—"

Dylan cleared his throat. "The last woman I courted had a white, fluffy cat named Tulip. Dreadful creature." But he leaned over toward Dishonor. "We're done talking about cats."

Dishonor touched his cuts again. "Fine. Let's talk instead about the fact that the thieves have discovered me, my secret storage facility, and possibly my identity. Though, Mr. Taber clearly didn't know it, and I only pray that they've not discovered who I am when I'm not at Carrington Shipping. I've no choice but to shut the two compromised lines down and let the drivers go, though I have no idea if they're actually involved."

Dylan pinched the bridge of his nose. "You heard Taber. Shutting down the lines could create a large disturbance."

Eliza drew in a deep breath. Her first concern was Dishonor, of course. But then she realized this could impact her too.

She'd been there today. Seen by Mr. Taber at the secret warehouse. She slid her fingers from the cat and slipped them into Dylan's grasp.

He laced his hand into hers.

But Dishonor grunted. "You think I should allow these men to continue stealing from me?"

Bash scratched his chin, but Dylan cocked his head as he tried to put several pieces together. "You said you believe he's also stealing from the Crown. Why do you think that?"

"Two weeks ago, as I did a final check on a wagon load, I found two crates in the back with the Crown's seal. When I asked the driver, he'd no idea how they had gotten there. But they were headed to Dover."

"Did you look inside the crates?"

"Yes." Dishonor ran a hand through his hair. "Exotic spices, silk, goods from the Orient mostly."

Bash's gaze lit with inspiration. "If you can prove that your books are off, do you think the Crown could as well? Prinny's got significantly more resources than we do to run an investigation."

"And more power to put a stop to whoever is at the top of this league of criminals," Dylan added.

Dishonor shook his head. "I've no relationship with the Crown." His voice tightened, growing harder and Eliza squinted her eyes, trying to assess his features in the growing darkness.

But Bash waved his hand. "Leave that to me. He's my second cousin on my father's side."

"All right. If you need to contact me, leave a note with the solicitor." And then Dishonor tapped the wall behind him as the carriage drew to a stop.

Bash raised his brow. "We can continue this conversation in my office."

Dishonor gave his head a shake. "Forgive me, Your Grace. But I think it best we spend as little time together as possible."

"But we now own a business together."

"True. But I don't have a wife or young ladies in my charge. We'll keep most of the attention on me for now. We don't want…" and then he stopped, giving Eliza a long look.

She gave a single nod. He was trying to protect her and her sisters still. "Thank you, Dishonor."

The carriage had stopped, and he snapped open the door, and then jumped out, disappearing into the night.

"He's gone again," Eliza said as Bash closed the door.

"Did you learn anything in the warehouse? And who was the Scot he was with?" Dylan asked as soon as the carriage started moving again.

"The warehouse is where he keeps several shipments of goods that only he and a few other trusted men in his business ever see or touch. And the other man wished to remain anonymous for now, but I have my suspicions."

Eliza's hand tightened in Dylan's. "Should we be concerned?"

"I don't think so, but I'm going to check in with my friend, the Earl of Goldthwaite. The first time I met Dishonor, I asked Goldthwaite to investigate Dishonor's real identity. It's time I circle back to see if he's learned anything," Bash said as he shook his head. Then he gave them both a long stare in the dark. "But we won't have any more information there until I've talked with Goldthwaite, which means it's time to discuss another pressing topic."

"What's that?" Eliza asked, nibbling on her lip.

Bash dropped his chin. "Your future marriage."

Oh. That.

Dylan gave Bash a hard glare.

Though he appreciated his friend's position, this was between himself and Eliza. "Once we've returned to your home, may I request an audience with Miss Carrington?"

Bash let out a breath, or perhaps a short laugh. "Fine, but it will be chaperoned. Unlike the last one."

Eliza straightened. "Don't be absurd. I just—"

Bash thumped his hand on the seat. "If you would like a choice in this engagement, you will allow the meeting to be chaperoned. Honestly, Eliza, I have attempted to give you a great deal of leeway in this matter, but you'd push a man past reason."

Eliza shrugged. "Why, thank you."

Bash made a choking sound, but Dylan grinned. "It's been a long day. Everyone is tired."

Bash shook his head. "The world has turned upside down. I was a man who cared about nothing and no one because I never took a thing seriously. Now, I am the enforcer and Menace is the voice of calm reason?"

That made everyone laugh.

They finished the ride in silence and then stepped inside only to find the other three Carrington sisters anxiously awaiting their arrival.

It took over an hour to update her sisters and then finally, Dylan found himself sitting across from Eliza with only Isabella tucked into the corner as a chaperone. Eliza's sister was doing a fine job of paying rapt attention to her embroidery, the swish of her needle poking through the fabric the only sound filling the silence.

Eliza rolled her eyes but said nothing about the addition.

He cleared his throat. He'd been waiting for this meeting all night and yet, he hadn't a clue where to begin.

Eliza scooted to the edge of her chair. She still wore a shirt, jacket, and trousers, and Dylan had the distinct urge to pull her into his lap without the hindrance of skirts and petticoats.

"About your proposal." She folded her hands. "Are we agreed to amend the clause about intimacy?"

Isabella's needle stopped, but Eliza kept her gaze fixed on his.

Dylan let out a long breath. He should keep his distance. If they were going to lead separate lives, they shouldn't get so intimately involved. But then again, as he stared at her, he knew he'd never be able to keep his hands off her when she was ensconced under his roof.

"That plan presents several problems, which I've already stated." He clenched his jaw. This conversation was proving difficult with an audience. He'd like to just spell every point out. "You could become pregnant. I could…" His teeth ground together. *I could fall in love.* He knew there were ways to avoid Eliza carrying his child, such as the use of French Letters. But feelings, that was a more difficult obstacle to overcome.

His chest tightened as he stared at her.

But her smile was soft. "We'll deal with each challenge as it comes. Just like we did today." She reached out and clasped his hand. "I find we make a rather excellent team."

He gave a single nod. They did make a good team. But, considering what he'd just realized, being a team didn't seem nearly enough.

He wanted her heart.

And he'd proposed a match of convenience. He shook his head, more to himself. This was why he always failed. Because now he'd gone and trapped himself into a match of unrequited love.

A day ago, she hadn't wished to marry him at all. That almost seemed better. At least then he'd have a chance to recover.

But now he'd be tied to a woman who saw him as a means to an end.

A chance to exercise her passion. Well, that had its perks.

But also, an opportunity to taste freedom. He was about to commit to a woman, a woman whom he'd fallen in love with, whose goal was to climb on a ship and leave him behind.

Damn he was a fool. Always.

"So…" She pressed her lips together. "It's decided then. We'll marry?"

"Yes. It's decided." He let go of her hand. He'd marry her. What else could he do? She needed him and… his heart twisted. This was going to hurt.

CHAPTER THIRTEEN

Eliza sat in the dark carriage listening for the subtle sound of someone approaching. She'd been sitting in the dark and cold for a quarter hour at least.

She needed to have a private conversation with Dylan and that wasn't going to happen in Bash and Isabella's home.

And much to her dismay, she didn't even know where Dylan lived.

Odd, considering she'd just agreed to live there too.

But that left her with few options for finding him alone.

And so she'd returned to her last trick. Sneaking into the carriage. At least this time, she waited inside the vehicle rather than riding on the back. That had been rather cold.

Footsteps on the cobblestone alerted her someone approached and so she pushed deeper into the shadows in case it wasn't Dylan.

But as the door snapped open, it was her soon-to-be husband who climbed in.

"Dylan." She quickly moved into the light again.

He started, swearing under his breath. "You scared me."

"I'm sorry." Not sure what else to do, she scooted across the carriage and settled herself next to him. Somehow, it would be easier to talk if they were touching. "But I needed to talk to you and—"

But she never got the words out. His lips came down on hers, taking her mouth in a scorching kiss that left her breathless.

She wrapped her arms about his neck as she pulled him even closer and in response, he tugged her into his lap, slanting her mouth open and ravaging her mouth with his.

Dylan surrounded her every sense, the feel of his muscular legs under the back of hers, the press of his chest, the touch of his mouth, his smell, the low rumble he made as their tongues came together.

Eliza was lost.

Every word she'd wished to say had left her head with the exception of one. She was glad she'd insisted on this dark meeting in the carriage. Because she'd never experienced anything like it.

This was better than any adventure she'd ever imagined in her life. The rush of her blood pounded in her ears as he flicked open her jacket and ran a hand down over breast.

She arched her back into the touch wanting more. Wanting all of him.

"My lord," the driver called. "Are you ready?"

Dylan ripped his mouth away. "Go."

The reins snapped and the carriage lurched forward, crushing them together. Eliza didn't complain. In fact, she wanted to be closer.

"Eliza," he rumbled again. "What did you wish to talk about?"

"Talk?" she replied, giving him a lingering kiss before she continued. "I've completely forgotten."

He chuckled then. "My home isn't that far so we've only got the trip there and then the return trip here to discuss whatever you wish to say."

"Return?" She didn't wish to return tonight. She wasn't sure she wanted to go back ever. With startling clarity she realized that remaining in his arms was her future.

Their marriage of convenience was proving very convenient indeed. More than convenient.

She pulled back to look in his eyes. She loved him. She wished to be next to him always.

And then her insides twisted in pain. But he wanted her inheritance. Not her.

He'd been painfully clear on that front.

Still. They were to wed, and she would approach his feelings like she did everything else. She'd create a plan of attack and convince him to want her…not just her money.

And it started by staying right here in his arms.

"You have to go back, Eliza. Bash would have my head."

She kissed him again, long and lingering and full of all the passion that had been building slowly inside her…until she met Dylan. And then it grew rather quickly. "Do we really care about Bash…" She kissed him again, sliding her hands into his hair.

"No." he replied as he caressed her front, cupping one of her breasts. "But I do care about you. You should be tucked in Bash's house. Where you belong. Where you are safe. And I wouldn't want to worry anyone. Not with everything that's happened."

She sighed. That was decidedly smart. "Now who's making responsible decisions?"

He chuckled against her lips even as his thumb flicked over her nipple, causing it to pucker against the chemise she wore under her dress.

She wished there could be less clothing between them. She wanted to feel his hands on her skin.

He slid his hand further down to her waist and then over her hip, trailing down the length of her leg until he reached her ankle.

He circled the slender part of her leg, giving a light squeeze before he skimmed his hand under her skirts and up her leg.

She gasped, the touch light and easy but somehow wreaking havoc with her senses. The higher he climbed the more desperate she became for…more.

"I haven't been the purest man," he whispered, trailing kisses behind her ear. "Like I said, I haven't made the best choices. But there are some advantages to all that experience, and I intend to share one of those with you right now."

"Yes," she gasped, so ready, she felt as though…she might come undone if he didn't touch her more.

And then his fingers reached her apex and he parted the fabric of her pantaloons giving her curls the lightest brush with his fingertips.

She jolted in sensation. How could something so small as that touch create such a strong reaction? A riot of feeling coursed through her body. She'd like to ask him, but he'd begun kissing her again, murmuring against her lips.

Then he slanted her mouth against hers, his tongue tangling with hers even as he touched her with more presser against her most intimate flesh.

She nearly broke apart and cried out, the intensity of the sensation taking her breath away.

"That's it, love," he crooned, starting a light rhythm that had her gripping his shoulders for support.

She wanted to cry out, she wanted to beg for more, she wanted…

But she lost the thought because suddenly her body spasmed, the intense pleasure shattering.

He smiled against her lips. "You are so beautiful, Eliza."

Her breath caught as she continued to hold onto him. She realized his other arm had wrapped tightly around her back, securing her weight. She was cradled against him, supported. She'd given herself over to him entirely and he'd made her sing with pleasure. "That was…"

He shook his head as he kissed her lips again. "I understand."

She blinked, realizing the carriage had come to a stop. "Where are we?"

"My home." He wrapped on the front of the carriage. "I need to return to Devonhall's," he called out.

The carriage started again.

Eliza huffed out a breath but didn't bother to sit up. She'd never been more comfortable. "But don't I get to see my future home?"

He cocked a brow. "Home? Aren't you going off on your adventures?"

There was something in his voice, the way it sounded. Hurt? She thought about going to America. That suddenly didn't seem half as interesting as staying right here. In England. London. This carriage. His arms. "And leave you and Bash to solve this mystery on your own? I don't think so."

But suddenly all the topics she'd wished to discuss came flooding back. What would their marriage be like? How did he feel about her? A sick knot formed in her stomach. She'd wished she asked these questions before he'd touched her because now…she felt raw and vulnerable in his arms and she hated that feeling. It reminded her of how she'd been when her father had left.

She didn't wish to be that person.

Not ever again.

DYLAN SENSED A SHIFT IN HER. Not long ago, Eliza had been like pudding in his hands. Now, he felt her stiffen.

She didn't like to be left out of anything.

"I would never dare solve it without you," he answered against her temple. "I simply thought that going to America was your plan." His eyes closed as she relaxed again. Not as fully but he was glad she'd stayed in his arms.

How did he tell her that she belonged with him? Not on some grand adventure but right here with him.

Then again, he wouldn't mind going off with her. Just as long…as long as they were together.

Would that anger her? She was fiercely independent. He didn't wish to suffocate her, just…just be with her. Next to her.

"I wouldn't go anywhere until I knew my sisters were absolutely safe," she replied.

"Of course." It was his turn to tense. Because once this was all done, once they'd figured out who threatened her family, they could figure out, well, them. Where did he stand? What did her future look like? Could he be part of it?

Part of him wanted to tell her how he felt. That he was in love with her, but right now, as they tried to keep her family safe, that felt selfish.

He'd solve this mystery and then he'd convince her to have not just a marriage of convenience, but one where they shared their lives and her adventures.

He grinned against her hair. He could picture her on the deck of a ship in men's pants, firing off orders. She'd be glorious.

"We've yet to decide any details for our wedding," he said rather than say any of the other thousand thoughts running through his head.

"No." She smiled at him then. "We haven't."

"Well?" He raised an eyebrow. "What are you thinking?"

Her tongue darted out and she licked her lips. "I wasn't. I'll let Isabella or Emily decide."

That made him wince. Shouldn't the bride care about the details of the wedding?

"But I am curious. What you just did to me. Is there a male equivalent? Can I do that to you?"

All thoughts of the wedding and even his hurt feelings left his head at those words. "Eliza," he started, just picturing her hand down his trousers made him hard as stone. Hell, he'd been like granite since the day he'd met her.

She started at his collarbone and began sliding her hand along his chest. "You're going to have to help me with the falls of your breeches. I couldn't get my own trousers off tonight."

Just remembering those trousers had him groaning as he pulled at the buttons, loosening his stays. She caressed lower still, across his stomach as his manhood strained against the fabric still covering him.

But when she finally moved past his shirt and touched his bare skin, he moaned as he felt the warm silkiness of her palm against his flesh.

And then her fingertips were sliding up his staff as light as his had been. Damn her but she was a quick study, already mimicking his touch.

"Eliza," he said, his voice rough. "There's no need to be gentle. I swear, I might explode from wanting."

"Shhhh," she replied and then lightly kissed a trail against his neck. "I've never touched a man before and I want to enjoy every second."

His eyes slid closed as she wrapped her hand about him. What was it about knowing that this was only for him, that she had only ever touched him?

And then his eyes snapped open. They'd made a business arrangement. Did that mean she'd be with other men while she was off seeing the world?

He let out a growl of dissention and her hand stilled. "Did I do it wrong?"

No. She'd touched him exactly right. And he had absolutely no intention of allowing her to touch another man. Ever.

He wrapped his hand about hers and slowly began working it up and down his staff. "No. Your touch is perfect."

"Your skin is like velvet. Does every man feel like this?"

Another grumble rolled deep in his throat. "I wouldn't know," he answered between clenched teeth.

She gave him the smallest squeeze. "Are all men this thick? You're rather well…"

Now that he didn't mind discussing at all. "No. They're not. And I have it on very good authority that a member like mine feels particularly enjoyable." There. She needn't think of other men at all.

Her eyes widened and she stalled underneath his hand. "You've been with a great many women. Haven't you?"

He could have cursed himself out as he felt her start to pull away. He held her hand in his. "Eliza," he rasped, trying to keep a clear head. "Not like this. Not like you."

She softened and her hand began to move again. "You mean that?"

"Every word and a great deal more that I am not saying because…" He stopped, realizing how much he was revealing. But with her touching him like this, he couldn't hold back.

"What aren't you saying?" she gasped. Their hands were moving together again, and a buzzing kept his brain foggy. He couldn't think.

"That I don't want a sham marriage."

"Oh," she said, stilling again.

A protest rumbled in his chest. "I want a real one. With you."

"Oh!" she said again. "Well that does change things."

How? How did it change things precisely? Was he a fool?

CHAPTER FOURTEEN

ELIZA STARED at him as warmth spread through her. She was holding his manhood in her hand as he confessed that he wished for more out of their relationship. "I want more too."

She felt him swell in her hand, her fingers barely able to fit all the way around him. Excitement pulsed through her at the feel of him in her hand. So warm and hard and vibrant.

"What do you want?" he asked and began moving her hand along his staff once again. Slowly this time.

She straightened, not letting go, but wanting to be level with his eyes when she said the next words. "I want to explore…" She drew in a deep breath as she felt him tense. Her legs had settled on either side of his as their chests touched, both their hands still on his staff between their bodies. "You."

That made him chuckle. Low and deep, it rumbled through her. Delicious. "I want to explore you too. But Eliza, it's more than just physically. That's what I meant when I said you were different. I feel things for you that…"

"Really?" Her other hand came to his cheek, cupping his face in her palm. "You do?"

"I do."

"I feel things for you too," she sighed, touching her forehead to his. "I think that I'm in love—"

He pulled her closer, kissing her with a fire that left her breathless. "You stole my line."

Her breath caught as the carriage rolled to a stop. "What?"

"Eliza," he whispered against her lips. "I'm in love with you too. I can't say when it happened, but I know that I feel it."

Her heart pounded against his chest matching his beat for beat. This was what she had wanted. She smiled to herself. Well, to be honest, she'd wanted something different entirely, but since meeting him, her goals had changed. And he suited them perfectly. He was a partner. A man who wanted her, loved her, and who understood she didn't wish to be left in the background but by his side on the forefront. "I feel it too."

The carriage rolled to a stop. He heard the footman jump down and give a theatrical cough outside the door. "We're here, my lord."

He slid her hand off his member and closed the falls of his breeches.

Eliza frowned. She didn't want to leave him now. They hadn't finished their conversation and she certainly wasn't done touching him.

He snapped the door open and then helped her out, following behind her. Then he turned to the driver. "Return just before dawn, if you please."

"Of course, my lord," the man answered and to his credit, his eyebrows only rose the smallest bit. Then he snapped the reins and drove off into the night.

"Dawn?" she asked, wrapping her arms about his waist.

He settled her close. "That's right. I'm relying on you to get me into the house without being caught."

"Hmmm. How do you feel about climbing garden trellises?"

He wrinkled his nose. "I'd break my neck."

She gave him a look up and down. "I think you could do it, personally."

"How about we try sneaking up the back stairs first?"

She laughed, burying her forehead into the crook of his neck. "Very well. But if you get caught, you're walking home and it's a cold night."

He snorted even as he squeezed her close. "Which is better? Freezing to death or falling to my death?"

She lifted her head. "This is fun. Is this what marriage will be like? How interesting. I'd prefer falling. Quicker."

They started moving toward the back door. "Really? So violent." But he quieted as they approached the door. Eliza peeked in to see the cook still at the stove but her back was to them. Eliza waved him on. He let her go and tiptoed into the stairwell disappearing around the corner just as Eliza closed the door.

"Hello," Cook said as she looked at Eliza. "I just heard a carriage."

A bit of a thrill raced down her spine. This *was* exciting. "I was saying goodnight to my fiancé before he left."

Cook nodded. "Congratulations." Then she turned to Eliza. "Would you like a cookie or two before bed? I just baked them for tomorrow. Ginger."

"Yes," came a whisper from the stairwell.

She nearly rolled her eyes even as she smiled. "That would be lovely. Thank you."

Then, grabbing the cookies, she started up the stairs after Dylan.

He ate both cookies before they'd even made it to her room. "You know, it takes away a bit of the fun out of espionage with you eating like that," she said as she closed the door.

He gave her a devilish grin. "Don't worry, love. I'm just preparing for the night ahead."

A jolt of awareness passed through her. "Give me that last piece of cookie," she said as she tried to snatch the gingerbread from his hand.

He pulled his hand away and then grabbing hers, tugged her close. Then, gently, he placed the cookie in her mouth. She took a bite, aware of the brush of his fingers on her lips, the feel of his body, the warmth of his ginger scented breath on her cheek.

The gingerbread, still warm from the oven, melted in her mouth. "Delicious," she murmured once she'd swallowed the delicate bite.

He'd already begun undoing the row of buttons at her back. "It was. But I bet it won't taste nearly as good as you."

She gasped in a breath even as he tugged off the top of her gown, then kissed her exposed collarbone.

Dropping down to his knees, he worked off her skirts, kissing her wrists, her palms, each of her fingertips. And when she'd been stripped to nothing but her chemise, he stood again, making quick work of his clothing until only his breeches remained.

Eliza swallowed a lump as she stared at his broad shoulders and narrow waist, muscles rippling as he moved. "You lied."

He stared at her, cocking his head to the side. "About what?"

She reached out a hand and trailed it along the ridges of his muscles. "You're completely capable of climbing the trellis."

He gave a soft laugh then. "I'll save those sorts of activities for when we're off on some adventure."

That made her melt. "Oh. I love that idea. You and I adventuring together."

"Of course," he softly replied. "I know the woman I'm marrying."

He did. And she loved him all the more for it. "This is our first great adventure."

Hells bells, she was glorious.

Gently, he pulled the pins from her hair, letting the dark tresses cascade down her back.

He'd never undressed a woman like this.

Passion, hot and deep, was burning in him, but he'd kept his movements gentle and easy. This was a moment he wanted to cherish. Remember forever.

He'd never expected to be here in his life. He rarely did things right, but deep in his soul, he knew Eliza was the best choice he'd ever made, and he absolutely would not ruin this by rushing.

A little voice in the back of his head said he'd find a way to wreck their marriage the way he destroyed everything else, but he beat it back down. Not tonight. Not here.

Right now, he'd cherish this woman with all the emotion he held in his heart.

He was back on his knees and she stared down at him, her gaze dark and wanting as her hands combed through his hair.

He reached for the hem of her chemise and skimmed the fabric up her legs.

When he'd gathered the material at her waist, he kissed her bare belly and felt her shiver. But he kept going, peeling the last barrier between them up and over her head.

She was stunning. His chest ached to look at her. Full breasts and hips were accentuated with a tiny waist. A woman had never made him ache like this and he stared, just wanting to commit her body to memory.

"Dylan." She lifted her arms to him. "I'm cold."

How could he deny a plea like that? He pulled her into his arms, lifting her feet off the ground and carrying her to the bed. As he set her down, he kissed her, pressing his weight on top of hers to warm her.

And then he slid his mouth lower, down her neck and across her chest.

He wanted to taste every inch of her. Slowly, he tasted each breast, counted her ribs with his lips, explored her stomach and then her hips.

As he parted her legs, he nibbled at her thighs, her breath coming in short gasps.

He rumbled out his own need, her center hot and ready for him. But he didn't slide up her body. Instead, he kissed her again, in her most intimate place, her heat and scent wrapping around him.

She cried out, her hands tugging at his hair.

He started a rhythm with his tongue as tension built within her. He could feel it as her thighs tightened about his head, her body clenching around his finger as he slid the digit inside her.

She was so close, and it made everything male in him want to roar with victory, but he slowed his touch even as she whimpered out a protest.

He had a better goal in mind.

CHAPTER FIFTEEN

ELIZA COULD FEEL that sweet tension building in her once again.
She wanted him, wanted him to finish her. She wanted...
Even more of his skin on hers.
And as though he were reading her mind, he climbed up her body, kicking off his breeches, his gaze hot and intense.
She wanted to touch him again. She'd love the feel of his manhood, but before she got the chance, he pressed his rod against her opening. White-hot desire pulsed through her.
She wrapped her arms about his back and urged him closer. She wanted more.
He began to slide deeper inside her as his finger had done moments before, but this felt different.
She stretched, a slight burning covering the pain.
"Does it hurt?" he asked, kissing her face between each word.
"Yes," she gritted out.
"I haven't fully seated myself—"
But she squeezed him. "Do it. Quickly." She'd never been one to shy away from anything and she wouldn't now.
He obeyed without question and gave a quick push all the way inside her.

There was a burst of pain but satisfaction too. They were together. Completely.

"Eliza," he rasped against her ear. "Are you all right?"

Emotion rolled over her in pleasant waves. Despite the pain, she was. "I'm wonderful."

He gave a short quiet laugh. "Not what most women say, I'd imagine."

She pressed her cheek to his. "Thank you for listening to me without question. I needed that to be quick."

He'd held still deep inside her but at that, he leaned back. "I trust you more than I trust myself."

They had to work on that, she quietly amended. He'd given her what she needed, a seat next to him. But him...he needed to learn to trust himself. And he needed a family who didn't tear him down but built him up. She would be that family. "I trust you too. Completely."

He drew up on his arms, looking down at her. "Eliza." Her name was rough as he looked at her a mixture of pain and pleasure etched on his strong features. "Be careful..."

"I won't," she said, pulling his head back. "It's you and me now. Always."

"But you've family depending on you." His face tightened.

"And now, they'll depend on you too."

In response, Dylan pressed down against her chest again, slowly pulling out of her body and then pushing back in. It didn't hurt nearly as much.

When he did it a third time and then a fourth, pleasure began to replace the pain and soon they were moving together in a rhythm that left them both breathless.

She held him tight to her chest as sweet tension built.

Words flitted in and out of her thoughts. *Love, trust, need, fulfillment* —but she couldn't seem to form them into coherent thoughts that could be spoken out loud so instead she held him tighter and whispered his name over and over until she finally crashed over the edge of her passion.

He didn't make it but a few more strokes before he cried out, his body shaking with his own release.

As he collapsed on top of her, she snuggled deeper into him. A contentment like she'd never known settled over her and as she drifted off to sleep, she realized there was nowhere else she'd rather be. She was home.

Eliza woke before the sun, warm and so cozy in her bed.

She smiled and glanced over at the pillow next to her only to find it empty.

Reaching out her hand, it was still warm. But Dylan was gone.

Where was he?

Had he left without waking her and saying goodbye? She sat up. His clothes were gone and hers were neatly stacked on her dressing table except for her chemise, which lay on the foot of the bed.

Something heavy settled in her stomach. Where had he gone?

DYLAN SAT on the seat of a carriage as the morning sun burned off the fog from the night.

He was trying to shake the feeling in the pit of his stomach that he'd just made a series of terrible decisions.

The feeling wasn't going anywhere.

Because he'd risen after a few hours of sleep and watched Eliza. Her face had been so relaxed, near angelic.

He'd risen and carefully folded her clothes. Then he'd dressed, all the while thinking about their future.

She loved him and he loved her. His chest still ached from it. But he had to prove to her that he was the sort of man she could trust.

He'd help her with her problems, with her sisters, and... That had been sound thinking in the wee hours of the morning. He'd decided to see the king.

Bash was right. It was the only way to move forward with the investigation. He knew he should wait for Bash. He was the one who'd seen the books and could prove the theft, but Dylan needed to know that he was actually a help and a true asset to Eliza and her family.

And this trip to see the king was not the adventure part. This was the sit-for-hours-in-a-salon-and-hope-the-king-might-give-an-audience piece. Surely, Eliza wouldn't mind that? Or at least, that's what he'd been thinking.

And by meeting the king, he'd add value to Eliza's life. But a nagging doubt had begun to whisper in the back of his mind. Perhaps he should have asked her first? He'd wanted to triumphantly return to her side. He pictured delivering news that would help them sweep to her sisters' rescue. But in the cold light of morning, he wondered...

Dylan had attended a Christmas party at the palace a few years back. He'd had a nice conversation with the king.

Which had led him to believe perhaps he'd be received.

Now, today, several hours later, as he made his way to the docks, he felt a surge of triumph along with a smidgeon of worry. Amazingly, he'd been seen.

Even more surprising, the king was aware of the theft and had come to the same conclusion, he needed to follow one of his compromised lines of goods. For him, goods he imported were said to have arrived but never seemed to make it to the palace.

But unlike Dishonor, the thieves had no idea that the king had suspicions. And with a shipment arriving at the London docks that very morning...instead of sitting in a salon all day, he'd sent Dylan to oversee its arrival.

Which was ridiculous.

Chances were the goods were gone already.

And Dylan had never run a shipping company before. How would he even know?

He needed Bash or Dishonor. Or Eliza.

And she was going to be furious when she realized he'd acted unilaterally. Why had he done this?

As usual, he was in over his head.

He sat next to a steward, who had not spoken a word since they'd left the palace, as they moved through the city toward the docks.

Finally, the man looked over at him. "Do you know anything about checking in crates?"

"No," he answered truthfully.

"Then why do you think you're here?"

He scratched his chin. "I'm not certain."

The steward huffed out a quick breath. "Forgive me, my lord, but why would the king ask you to come on this trip if you did not serve a purpose?"

"Well, I'm about to marry into a shipping company being attacked by the same thieves."

"Do you recognize any of them?"

"A few, actually." He didn't bother to mention those men were all in custody and being questioned by the Bow Street Runners.

"What I could use..." The steward curled his lip. "Is a man who can tell if the captain or any of his crew are lying to me."

"Oh," he turned to look at the man then, a smile spreading across his lips for the first time all morning. "In that case, I run a gaming hell. And I pride myself on sensing when a man is bluffing. I'll do my best to help you on that account."

The steward smiled back. "Well, then. Excellent."

But an hour later, he was growing defeated. It seemed as if every crate was there, every man accounted for, and every crew member genuinely eager to please the king. He leaned over the side of the rail, his hands resting on his head. His big grand gesture was turning into a dud.

Eliza would be furious, and he didn't even have good news to soften her irritation. He should have left a note. But truly, he hadn't been able to find parchment or quill and he'd assumed he wouldn't be that long. Which was always his folly. Not thinking all the details through.

And then he saw something.

A rowboat tied just off the side of the ship with three small crates loaded in it. They had the logo of the Crown and Chinese symbols on the sides.

In the congestion of the Thames, the two men in the boat were silent and as they loaded a fourth crate into their little boat, another man jumped from the ship into the rowboat and untied the rope holding it to the ship.

The man who'd jumped in turned toward Dylan and that's when he realized it was the exact same Scot he seen with Dishonor yesterday. Surprise and anger coursed through him.

"Bullocks," he said through clenched teeth as he started moving through the back of the ship.

The theft had happened in a matter of seconds and everyone was so busy…was he the only one who'd noticed?

But by the time he'd made it to the back of the boat, they were already rowing away.

Damn. His hands itched with the need to do something. He'd lose the Scot. Did he jump in the water?

Find a boat to follow?

The Scot looked up and the two men's gazes collided.

The Scot stared for a second before he held a single finger to his lips and then continued rowing.

Dylan blew out a frustrated breath and then he realized… Dishonor would know where to find the man.

If they could trust Dishonor at all. What did they know about the man besides the fact he'd saved the girls once? Then he let out a short cry of frustration. That was something.

What did he do?

Running his hand through his hair, he knew.

He went to Eliza and Bash. They'd surely be able to help him.

If Eliza didn't kill him, or worse, end their engagement.

Fear rippled through him. Perhaps he should chase the thieves instead. They'd likely be kinder than his fiancée. How mad would she be that he'd gone off without her?

CHAPTER SIXTEEN

Eliza had paced for much of the morning, wringing her hands and obsessively looking at the clock on the mantle.

Because she couldn't tell Bash what she'd done last night, she didn't know how to say that something was wrong.

Dylan had left. After confessing his love. Why?

She had asked Bash at breakfast where Dylan lived but the other man had only chuckled. "You'll know soon enough. I hope you're up for the redecoration. It's going to be a big job."

She'd waved her hand. "Emily will help me. I'm more concerned about where he might be right now. He'd said he'd come." She grimaced at the lie, but Bash didn't seem to notice.

"I'm sure he'll be here soon. It is only eight in the morning. How early did he say he'd arrive? If you'll excuse me, I'm off to write a letter to the king requesting an audience. It's time we started getting some answers."

That should make her feel better. Answers were what they needed. But as she'd watched Bash leave, worry still filled her belly.

It felt an awful lot like when she'd written to her father. The multiple letters he'd never replied to. This is why she'd wanted to be alone.

But all she could do was wonder about Dylan. Sick dread filled her stomach. Why would he have left this morning? After everything they'd shared.

She'd paced for close to two hours before she'd returned to Bash's office. She needed to know where he was. She couldn't stand the worry another moment. Why hadn't he left a note, or something, to tell her where he'd gone?

When she knocked, Bash called out immediately, but he sounded... distracted. Far away.

As she opened the door, she saw him scanning a letter.

Her brows drew together in question as Bash looked up at her. "Menace is a bloody idiot."

"What do you mean?" A lump clogged her throat as she pressed her hands to her cheeks.

"I mean, I've just received a missive from our king. Menace went to our sovereign without me and now our leader has sent him to oversee a shipment of goods likely being poached by the very smugglers who attempted to kill us yesterday."

"What?" Fear jolted through her, making her knees weak. Then, red-hot anger charged through her. Didn't he understand they were to make decisions together? Hadn't she been clear?

Because now she was home again, worried that another man she loved was gone forever and her only job would be to pick up the pieces once again.

"The fool," Bash hissed, rising.

She clenched her hands. "I completely agree. What are we going to do?"

"We?" Bash groaned as he came around the desk. "You can't come, Eliza. It's too dangerous."

"Give me two minutes so I can get my pistol," she said, spinning. "If you leave without me, I shall never forgive you."

"Eliza," he called after her. "Of course I am leaving without you. You can't keep coming on these things and Menace isn't here to protect you this time."

She frowned as she skidded to a stop. "Don't you understand Bash?

I've done nothing but wait for months. Wait and worry. Years, in fact, I watched my mother pine while I helped raise my sisters. They remember the times he was home, his arms full of gifts. But me? I remember the times he was away. The worry my mother held when she thought no one was looking. I can't be that person, Bash. I won't."

He looked at her, his lips drawn tightly. "I allowed your sister, my wife, to put herself in danger at that club. I hate that place, now, did you know that? I hate the idea of you getting hurt. And your father, he hated it too. That's why he didn't tell you so much. That's likely why he allowed Dishonor into his business. To help protect you. It's what men do for the women they care about."

"That might be true, but I am strong and capable, and I won't sit idly by as life happens to me. I'll make my own way or…" But those words were hollow. She wasn't making her own way any longer. It was their way. He'd forgotten that, though. "I'm scared for him."

"Don't be. I'm fine."

She spun around to see Dylan leaning against the wall.

Her fists clenched even tighter as she charged toward him. She was going to kill him.

Eliza looked…angry. Her fists were clenched, her chin set in a hard line, her eyes cold.

He'd been worried about this. Until he'd found useful information and then he'd been elated.

He'd come back and with information that would move them one step closer to solving this mystery.

But she didn't appear as though she wanted to hear his good news.

"Where have you been?"

Bash cleared his throat. "What time did you two set a meeting?"

"I needed to help you—"

"Help me?" He saw her throat working. "I believe I have been completely explicit about how I wanted you to help me."

He winced. She had him there. "But your sisters...they need—"

Once again, she did not allow him to finish. "Do not pretend this was about my sisters."

He pushed off the wall he'd been leaning on. No. It hadn't really. "I wanted to prove my worth."

She snorted. "Exactly. You wanted to prove something, but you left me here to worry and I hate that more than anything. I've explained to you why that is so."

She stopped a few feet in front of him, her arms crossing, and her chin angled up as she continued to glare.

"I didn't mean to—"

Her mouth dropped open. "You didn't mean to what? Do the one thing I asked you not to do? You went off to see the king, no less. A job Bash was handling and then gallivanted to the docklands on a covert mission to see the very man who tried to kill us yesterday—"

This time, he interrupted, irritation coursing down his spine. "Now you're worried about your own safety? You've been reckless, running headlong into danger since I first met you."

"That is my job in this family." Her voice was rising. "Since I was a child, I did all the things a father would do because he wasn't there to do them. I taught my sisters to climb trees, to fish in the country, I stood up to bullies, I ran headlong into danger to keep them from harm. It's my job to keep them safe. I thought you understood, I won't be a woman who sits at home and waits and worries. Not ever again."

He stepped closer. "I've allowed you to go on several of these—"

"Allowed?" she yelled over him. "You've allowed me?" She stepped closer and without warning gave him a hard push in the chest. He took a half step back steadying himself. "That's what is so infuriating. I don't need you to allow me...I have always been perfectly capable. And I don't need to do it alone, but you're not supposed to either. We're supposed to be a team."

He winced, realizing that his word choice had been poor. "Eliza. I know that. I wasn't trying to act unilaterally. I just wanted—"

"But you did. Act on your own. And I cannot marry a man who

wished to leave me at home to wait and to worry while he rushes headlong into danger."

What the hell did that mean? "You're not—"

"I am." She stood straighter. "I would like to dissolve our arrangement."

He reached out to her, but she took a step back. "But—" He looked up at Bash. Pain was lancing through his chest. She couldn't just end it, but she was.

He could say the words. That he'd compromised her last night. Bash would force the match. But even he understood how awful it would be to start a marriage like that. So instead, he dropped his hand. "I tried to warn you."

"Warn me of what?"

"I always do exactly the wrong thing," he said so quietly, that he wasn't even certain he'd uttered the words out loud. "My parents would tell you if they could. I find a way to muck up every relationship with my own actions."

Her eyes widened as she stilled. "That isn't…" But then she trailed off.

"It is," he replied. "And it's all right. I know it's my fault. The truth is, I just wanted to prove my worth to you. Help you save your sisters and clear a path for our own adventures. It was selfish of me. I know. I'm a selfish bastard. My mother would tell you that too."

She brought her hands up to cover her mouth, her eyes crinkling in pain at the corners. "Dylan."

But whatever else she was going to say was cut off as yet another visitor arrived.

A well-dressed young lady came flying down the hall in a flurry of skirts, the butler following close behind. "Madame," he called. "You must wait for an audience."

"I cannot," the woman cried.

"Avery?" Eliza asked, her brow furrowing. "What's the matter?"

Avery skidded to a stop. That's when Dylan realized she had the same rich brown hair and chocolate eyes as all the Carrington sisters.

"Oh, Eliza." The girl reached for Eliza, collapsing into her arms as she trembled, tears shining in her eyes. "It's Papa."

"What happened?" Eliza stepped up and embraced the other woman. "What's wrong with Uncle Malcolm?"

A sob ripped from the other woman's lips. "He's dead."

CHAPTER SEVENTEEN

SHOCK COURSED through Eliza like a wave.

If she were being honest, she'd wished for Uncle Malcolm's death on several occasions. But to hear the words out loud, she ached for her cousin. Her father was the only family Avery had. Besides Aunt Mildred, of course.

Eliza cringed as she looked back at Bash. With the imposter Aunt Mildred here in London, Bash would have no choice but to move Avery into the house.

In that moment, she actually felt sorry for Bash. She felt even more sorry for Uncle Malcolm, though the man had made his own bed, cavorting with thieves.

"Avery," she said, holding the other woman tighter. Whatever she felt on the inside, Avery deserved her empathy now. "I am so very sorry."

Avery gasped. "He was cruel. I know that. And he wasn't a particularly good father or husband. But after mother died," Avery hiccupped in the pause. "He was all I had."

"I know," Eliza shushed her softly, rubbing her back with her hand.

"Forgive my interruption," Bash said behind her. "But this is…"

"The Honorable Avery Winston," Eliza still held her cousin as she gave Bash a look that half pleaded and half grimaced. "The Baron of Pennington's daughter."

Bash let out a soft groan as he ran a hand through his hair.

Dylan looked on silently, his own features having gone hard as stone.

Eliza swallowed a lump.

He'd made an awful mistake going off like that. He should have told her. Included her. She'd been completely clear on that front.

But he'd been clear too.

He always made the wrong choice, or he thought he did. It had been her job to teach him that he made exactly as many wrong choices as everyone else. And she'd failed him too. Gone and berated him when she should have supported.

She'd been as wrong as he'd been.

Drat.

And now she held an absolute mess in her arms so she couldn't tell Dylan so.

In fact, just before Avery had arrived, she'd ended their engagement.

Double drat. She'd like to use a few words far stronger than that, but she broke enough social rules as it were.

Her cousin sobbed in her arms.

"Avery," she softly said as she continued to pat. "Let's go sit and then you can explain everything."

Avery nodded into her shoulder as they made their way into the library.

Eliza settled her cousin in a chair as she dabbed at her eyes. "There isn't much to tell. A Bow Street Runner arrived at the house an hour ago to say they'd found him with a knife in his back in the Thames." Avery continued to cry more quietly. "That's all he said. He didn't have any leads and said these sorts of cases were difficult to solve."

Eliza looked up to see Dylan and Bash exchanging a glance. "Bash," Eliza said as she straightened. "Would you get my sisters, please? And Aunt Mildred too. This is a conversation they should be part of."

Avery continued to sniffle as she turned to Dylan. "And if you would please—"

"I'm not leaving." He stood straighter. "Engagement or not, I said I would help, and I will."

She melted at those words. "I'm glad you're going to stay. Thank you."

He cocked his head to the side, assessing her as Bash left the room.

She couldn't say what she wanted to, and she needed to comfort Avery, but she also needed...well, she had to apologize.

Crossing the room she looked at Dylan, trying to convey with her eyes what she felt in her heart. "About what I just said..."

"We'll talk about it later," he answered. "Right now, focus on your cousin."

She gave a stiff nod as she returned to Avery's side.

But as her sisters arrived and Bash returned, she noted that Dylan and Bash had relegated themselves to a corner.

Leaving Avery in Isabella's capable hands, she approached the two men.

Without a word, Dylan held out his hand and placed an arm about her waist.

"What are we discussing?" she asked.

Bash ran a hand through his hair. "How what was front is now back and left is now right." His head dipped down and he looked...tired.

"What does that mean?" she asked, looking at Dylan.

Bash rubbed his forehead. "I just got a note from Goldthwaite. There is no Dishonor. I mean, it was a fictional name to begin with, but it turns out it's a fictional name to cover a fictional name."

"What?" Eliza gasped, covering her mouth with her hands.

"Your father's partner is listed as John Smith. And while thousands of John Smith's exist, none of them match our man. The partnership is a fiction."

She trembled as she placed a hand against the wall to steady herself. "No." Right about now, she wished for Dylan's strong arms to wrap about her.

He didn't touch her, however. Instead he shook his head. "It gets worse. I saw Dishonor's partner stealing from the king."

"Oh," she cried, her hands coming to her mouth.

"And he was at the Docklands...on the Thames. And if I were to guess, it was around the same time that your uncle..."

She clamped her hand tighter over her mouth to keep from making another sound but inside, she wanted to cry. She couldn't stand another moment and she pressed closer to Dylan who wrapped her tight in his embrace. "You don't think..."

"We don't know. Is Dishonor the thief? Stealing this whole time? Playing us?" Bash scrubbed the back of his neck. "Why is that with every piece of information we get, the situation worsens?"

"I don't know," she answered quietly. Then she took a deep breath. "Is it possible that Dishonor and this other man are just trying to catch the thieves like we are?"

"It's possible," Dylan answered. "But it's so hard to know."

"What do we do next?"

"We?" Bash asked, his voice dropping. "Eliza, I know you're still hurting from your father's disappearance but—"

Dylan looked down. "Is that why you want to be part of this? Because of your father's disappearance?"

She shrugged as her hand came to rest on his chest. "Partially. Even before that though..." She drew in a breath.

"If you'll excuse me," Bash said, giving them a sidelong glance. Apparently, he understood when they needed a moment alone. "I believe Isabella needs me."

The moment they were alone, she looked up at him. "Dylan. I'm sorry that I cancelled our wedding. I didn't mean it. And I shouldn't have been so angry. You found out useful information and what's more..."

He shook his head. "I shouldn't have gone off without telling you what I was doing. I wanted to help but even as I was doing it, I knew I'd made the wrong choice—"

She shook her head. "I understand. You want to do the right thing and I did exactly as your parents would have done."

He chuckled. The sound was sad as he dropped his forehead to hers. "I deserved your anger. That's the thing. I always deserve it."

"You don't. Though next time, we're going off together."

He nodded, holding her close. "From now on, I won't act without you."

"And I will trust in you. You did a wonderful job today, uncovering more information. The question is, what do we do with it?"

He looked over at Bash. "This is where I always get in trouble. My instincts tell me to run to Dishonor and demand answers."

She nodded. "What if we follow him? See if he meets up with the Scot?"

Dylan nodded. "Not a bad plan. Except we've no idea if he'll return to that warehouse or not."

"Could we leave a note with the solicitor?" She nibbled her lip.

"As a means to follow him? Maybe, though, then he'll know we're looking for him."

She sighed. "We could pack up my family and leave London."

"Also, not a bad plan. Though it doesn't protect your business."

"Our business. I know you need the revenue."

"I need you," he murmured. "Bash was right from the start. As long as I can pay the creditors, hang the rest."

She smiled. "All right. So we're getting married again and we agree to be a team. Let's see what Bash thinks we should do about our mystery."

"Good plan." He brushed a hand along her cheek. "I know today has been difficult, but I am also anxious for us to wed."

Those words made her forget some of her worry. "As am I. Can you get a special license so that we might have it done quickly?"

He leaned down then and kissed her. "I think that can be arranged."

"Dylan," she whispered, needing a bit of privacy in a crowded room. "I love you."

He slid his fingers down her neck to her shoulder. "I love you, too, Eliza."

She gave him a large open smile. "I'm glad we worked that out."

He chuckled. "Me too." Then he leaned down and whispered in her ear. "About that trellis…"

CHAPTER EIGHTEEN

IN THE END, they married three days later in a small ceremony with just their closest friends and family.

Eliza wasn't the sort of girl who'd pictured her wedding, but as she thought back, her fantasy would have been exactly what her actual wedding had been.

Quiet, intimate, and full of love. The soft glow of candles all about them as they said their vows.

Her sisters and cousin were there. And his friends. But that was it. They'd had a simple wedding breakfast and then they'd departed for his home.

It was one of the two properties he'd been bequeathed, and he hadn't been lying when he'd said it needed work. But it was going to be her home, and she loved it.

He hadn't even given her a tour as he carried her up the stairs and into the main bedroom and this time, there was nothing soft or gentle about the way they made love. They clung to each other as their bodies expressed the love in their hearts.

When they'd finished making love, they lay together. It was Dylan who broke the silence first. "Where shall our first adventure be?"

She laughed, lifting her head. "I'm fairly certain we're in the midst of the greatest adventure of our lives."

"True," he answered, stroking a hand down her back. "But you said you wished to travel and…" He gave her a long, slow kiss.

Eliza's heart hummed. "I did say that, didn't I?" She took a deep breath. "Truth be told, I do have a few ideas."

"Really?" He sat up, pulling her into his lap. "Do tell."

"How do you feel about France? Or India? Or the Orient?" She nibbled her lip as she watched his brow knit together in confusion.

"I'm not certain I understand? I thought you wished to see America?"

"I do." She drew in a breath. "You need a way to bring in revenue to rebuild the marquisate. I need to feel like I am not sitting at home. What do you think about taking the helm of my father's business? I know Bash doesn't want to run Isabella's share. And neither Emily nor Abigail have any interest. We could—"

But she wasn't able to finish. "You are the bravest, most intelligent, most beautiful woman I have ever met."

She smiled against his lips. "And I could never imagine doing something like this without you."

He reached for her hand, twining their fingers together. "I love you, Eliza, and now that we are together, I can't imagine my life without you. You make me…" he paused, leaning back to look in her eyes. "You make me a better man."

She reached up and ran her hand through his hair. "You make me better too, Dylan. I thought I wanted to walk this world alone on some great adventure, but it turns out, the fun is wherever you are."

He grinned as he kissed her again. She'd found her home.

A FORTNIGHT LATER…

. . .

DYLAN SAT behind a curtain at the Den of Sins, Eliza at one side, Bash at the other. He watched as Isabella, dressed as a man, dealt another round of cards. She'd been working the tables for a week in disguise.

The brown coat she wore made her shoulders appear larger and Abigail had dusted her face with ash to give her the appearance of whiskers.

"Dishonor hasn't come," Eliza whispered, tapping her foot. "This plan isn't working."

Dylan reached for her hand. He and Bash had been watching the warehouse, but they'd seen no sign of Dishonor.

Before Isabella and Bash had married, Isabella had worked here in disguise to keep her sisters fed. Dishonor had come here to give her money and they'd hoped he'd come again…

"Maybe he knows we're onto him," Bash growled. "When I get my hands on him."

"We don't know that he did anything," Eliza replied.

"You're right. It's just odd that he disappeared just as Dylan saw his partner stealing." Bash grunted. "And if I were honest, I want to take my frustration out on someone. He seems like a good candidate."

Dylan squeezed her fingers. "I totally understand. But I find it difficult to believe he's the thief. He saved the women, he told them of their inheritance. He might only come when the girls need him. Which, with us in their lives, they don't."

"The solicitor hasn't heard from him either. Not for days," Bash added with a frown.

"Thanks to the stewards," Eliza murmured, "shipments are going out. And he shut down those two lines like he said he would. I've triple-checked the books, the logs, and the actual shipments. No more goods or money is missing."

Dylan shook his head. "That can't be the end can it? We still don't know for certain who was behind anything. I told the king what I know, but I'm not able to actually identify either Dishonor or the Scot." He scratched his chin. "Perhaps they were behind it after all. Now that we're getting close, they've disappeared."

"Or." Bash looked at Eliza and frowned. He still had trouble speaking freely in front of her at times. "The Scot killed both Malcolm and Dishonor."

Eliza shivered next to him. "But he can't hurt us, can he? This Scot? He doesn't have access to the business?"

"Not that I can find in any of the paperwork," Bash said as he lifted the curtain a bit higher to watch Isabella. "So, perhaps, it really is over with. I hope Dishonor isn't dead, but I'd love to call this mystery closed. Your uncle is gone, the business isn't losing any more money, and—"

Then he stopped talking as his gaze swung toward the door. "Damn it all to bloody hell!"

Dylan followed Bash's eyes. Standing in the doorway in the Den of Sins was Dishonor. Bleeding. Badly.

"It's not over yet," Eliza said as she stood. Without another word, she linked her hand with his and raced from the hidden room and out onto the floor. They weren't done with their adventure, and he had the feeling Dishonor was about to play a key role. He looked at his wife; with her by his side he was ready for whatever the future would bring.

DUKE OF DISHONOR

January 1821
London

Emily Carrington sat in the parlor, well, one of many, at the home of the Duke of Devonhall. Her soon-to-be brother-in-law. She supposed this was about to be her sister's home too but as she looked around at the opulence, she couldn't quite believe it.

The past six months had felt like a nightmare…and then a fairytale. But that came later…

Emily's father ran a successful shipping company and he travelled often. Her chest tightened and she swallowed. At least, she hoped he still ran the shipping company. He'd left on a trip much like any other, well more than a year ago. Or had it been closer to two? It was hard to keep track with all the madness.

The real trouble began when their mother passed. As if such an event would not break the spirits of four young women, their father never came home. He didn't write to them, he didn't return, and they weren't even sure he was alive.

He usually travelled regular routes that allowed them, under normal circumstances, to communicate by letter. But they'd not heard a word in more than six months. Not since their mother's death.

Emily covered her mouth with her hand, ignoring the babble of her sisters in the background.

As if all this weren't enough, their uncle, the only male relative they had in England, had been systematically attempting to steal their father's shipping business for years.

Which meant, not only were they orphans, but they had to hide their father's disappearance from the one man who was supposed to help them.

She shivered in revulsion. Uncle Malcolm was supposed to protect them and instead he'd left them in a complete state of penury. They'd been defenseless and destitute. Alone and afraid.

She wrapped her arms about herself. Her sisters Isabella and Eliza had kept them fed, clothed, warm and now Isabella would surely marry a duke. They were saved.

What had Emily done all this time to help her family? Not a thing. Just two years younger than Isabella and three below Eliza, she might as well be a child, rather than a woman of twenty. She'd been at the mercy of the world and reliant on her sisters' wit and wiles while she'd been helpless.

She'd smiled and hugged in support as she'd allowed her two older, stronger sisters to face danger time and again while she stayed home to care for Abigail.

Isabella was exceptionally talented mathematically while Eliza was one of the bravest people she knew. What was Emily? Pretty, they said. Kind. But that wasn't special or interesting.

She sighed to herself as Isabella raced into the room where Emily sat with Eliza and Abigail, their youngest sister. Isabella was pale, a note clutched in her hand.

Eliza stood. "What's wrong?"

Emily's heart thudded in her chest as Isabella covered her mouth with one hand. Then she dropped it again. "There's been a fire. On one of Papa's ships. Bash wants us to meet him at our home." Then she cleared her throat. "I mean at father's home. This is our home now." And she gave a skeptical glance around the room.

The Duke of Devonhall had hired a woman to pose as their Scottish aunt in order to launch them into society and find them husbands. The imposter Aunt Mildred sat in a chair next to a fire, largely ignoring the girls. But at the mention of the duke, her head snapped up. Emily had to give the woman credit on one account. She was singularly loyal to her employer.

"Then let's go." Aunt Mildred waved her hand, gesturing them forward. "We mustn't keep His Grace waiting."

"I think this is a mistake," she whispered, her gaze narrowing. Just this morning the Duke of Devonhall told them not to leave the house. Their uncle had threatened to sell them at auction to the highest-bidding husband. She shuddered inwardly and a cold fist clamped around her heart. Not a fate she relished.

But her sisters were in a flurry of conversation and neither acknowledged nor heeded her comment. Perhaps they hadn't heard at all but a quarter hour later, they were all seated in the carriage, bustling off to their Cheapside home.

Her feeling of unease didn't lessen. In fact, her trepidation only grew. Why hadn't she tried harder to be heard?

Not sure what else to do, she reached for Isabella's hand, her eyes meeting her sister's. Why hadn't she objected more loudly? Insisted they stay home? Because she was meek, easing people's fears rather than acting on her own.

Isabella stared back. "We should stop," she said, squeezing Emily's hand. Then she banged on the wall and the carriage slowed. Isabella was the most like Emily and their thoughts were in line now. Emily sighed with relief, giving Isabella a nod of confirmation. This trip was a mistake.

"Isabella?" Eliza asked, looking over at her as the carriage slowed. "What is it?"

"This doesn't feel right," Isabella answered. "Something is off. I can feel—"

"Who are you and what do you want?" the driver called as the carriage lurched forward again.

The girls gasped and Isabella fell back into her seat even as Emily fell toward her, bracing herself on Isabella's legs.

"Stop that carriage or we'll shoot," a stranger's voice called.

Emily squeaked out a tiny scream, fear pounding through her veins. She clutched her sister's hand harder as she silently berated herself for not acting as she knew she should. Why hadn't she sounded an alarm sooner?

The carriage turned even as it picked up speed. They were clearly making a getaway and all the women tried to brace themselves as Eliza cried out when her head hit the wood frame.

Suddenly a shot rang out and the driver screamed. A thud followed and Emily squeezed her eyes shut. "Did someone just shoot the driver?" She asked but no one answered. The next series of questions, she kept to herself but inwardly, her thoughts spun. *Had he fallen? What was happening out there? Were random thugs attacking their carriage or was this the work of their uncle?*

"Come on out, ladies," the voice called again. The man's tone dripped with barely concealed irritation. "There is someone who'd like to visit with you."

Aunt Mildred let out a gasp. "This is not part of the job."

"Aunt Mil—"

She waved them off. "My name is Caroline. I quit."

"You're quitting now?" Eliza huffed as she grabbed up an umbrella, holding it in front of her like a sword.

Isabella straightened. "I accept your resignation. You may leave the carriage now."

Emily turned to glare at the older woman. So much for her loyalty to the duke. A chastisement rose to her lips but she pushed it back down. Her sisters had already done the job of expressing their dissatisfaction. Mildred, or Caroline, or whatever they were calling her, made no move to get out and instead, shrunk further into the bench.

Abigail gave a quick laugh as the older woman turned pale, but that voice called again. "If you're thinking you can escape, you should know there's a man out here for each of you to make certain you're escorted to your host."

"It was a trap," Eliza whispered. "That note wasn't from Bash, was it?"

Bash was the duke's nickname, one that suited him perfectly. Emily looked between her sisters, wondering how they might possibly get out of this mess. "I should have spoken up earlier. I knew this was a mistake but I…"

"No," Isabella answered. "I should have known. I've just never seen his handwriting."

Eliza frowned. "It's not either of your faults. But the question now is, do we stay in or get out as they're requesting?"

"Stay in," Abigail inserted. "Don't be a fool."

"But then they can just drive off with all of us in this carriage." Emily pointed out, lifting her finger in the air. Abigail gave her a look halfway between quizzical and irritated. Emily understood why. She rarely spoke up in these sorts of situations. But then again, not talking hadn't helped them at all. Look at where they were in this moment. If only she'd shared her fears earlier, perhaps they'd have been better off.

"Ladies," the voice called again. It held a sing-song quality that made Emily start in fear. "Time to come out."

"Eliza." Isabella turned to their eldest sister, her voice low. "One of us needs to climb out and make it to the driver's seat to get the carriage out of here."

"How close are the men? How many of them are there?" Eliza asked as she looked out the window.

Emily could see her sisters forming a plan. As usual, they were jumping to aid their family.

Shame washed through Emily. How could she allow them to put themselves in danger time and again while she stood on the sidelines? Because they'd always taken care of her, protecting her from harm. And yes. She appreciated their concern and love, but at twenty years of age, she was more than capable of assisting them. Now, more than ever, she wanted to find a way to prevent anything like what had happened after their mother died from reoccurring. She looked out her own window, trying to assess the danger. Trying to figure out a way to help.

Abigail peaked through one curtain. "I see two. Ten or fifteen paces away."

"I see three," Emily said. "Two further back and one right next to the door."

Eliza nodded. "Ok, I'll bash that one with my umbrella and then Isabella will climb into the driver's seat and whisk you all to safety before the others can reach us."

"But what if he grabs you?" Isabella asked.

Emily watched Eliza as cold fear flickered across her eldest sister's face before she carefully masked it. That was Eliza. Brave, bold, and willing to sacrifice for her family.

"I can't have you being the only hero," Eliza said as the door rattled. Any moment now their attacker would have the carriage door open.

Isabella tightened her grip on the door. "Eliza. You're not likely to climb back in if—"

"I'll be fine." Eliza grabbed the handle too. Then she whispered, "Get our sisters to safety and marry that duke. They need him and so do you."

Emily grabbed the handle too, pushing Eliza's hand away. Eliza could not sacrifice herself today, their sisters needed Eliza alive and well. Emily, with startling clarity, realized that she was completely dispensable. "Give me that umbrella." Then she snatched the pole from Eliza's hand. With a quick breath of air, she pushed the door open. "Now!" she yelled.

The door swung out and, with all three of their weights behind it, Emily felt the moment that the wooden panel hit the attacker.

He grunted, stumbling back and Emily jumped out, hitting him with the umbrella. The force of it rattled through her body, but she didn't stop as Isabella followed her out, scrambling to the front of the carriage and onto the seat. She saw other men rushing toward them, and her hands shook as she turned, wielding Eliza's umbrella like a sword.

But the first man had recovered, and he grabbed her from behind, holding her in his beefy grip. A scream ripped from her lips.

Eliza had also climbed out and jumped on the man's back, clawing at him and attempting to wrench Emily out of his grip. For her part, Emily tried to twist away but his hands were so strong she couldn't escape.

Another man barreled toward Emily and for a moment, another scream built in her throat. What would the two men do to her and her sister? How had she ever thought she was strong enough for this?

But this new man yelled, "Go!" And then he swung his fist, hitting the attacker with a force that sent the man sprawling to the ground. The hit jarred through Emily even as Eliza jumped out of the way.

Isabella gasped from the bench. "You!"

In an instant, their hero pushed Eliza through the open door, and she fell to the carriage floor. "Go!" he yelled again and then grabbed up Emily around the waist, clutching her to his chest as he reached for the back of the carriage.

Distantly, she heard Aunt Mildred give a shriek as Abigail leaned out and slammed the carriage door shut again.

Emily could barely register a detail except that the moment her body tucked against his, his strong arm circling her waist, she felt... safe. She wrapped her arms about his neck and tucked her head against his shoulder, completely protected by his large strong frame.

And then another emotion skittered down her back. He was lean and strong, and she looked up into his square jaw and penetrating eyes...he was sinfully handsome.

Dark hair ruffled in the breeze as the carriage began to move. The wind, bitingly cold, plucked at her cheeks but he pulled her closer to his body.

"Isabella," a voice rang out into the damp air. Uncle Malcolm. Emily would know the sound anywhere. "Come back here."

She didn't look back nor did she answer as the carriage picked up speed. She'd never look at or talk to that man again. Uncle Malcom was dead to her.

Another shot rang out and the man protecting her gave a grunt.

DUKE OF DISHONOR

Had he just been shot? Her hands tightened on his shoulders as she looked up into his face. "Are you all right?" she gasped, feeling his muscles under her fingers.

"I'm fine," he answered and for the first time, he looked down at her. His eyes were a hazel green and fringed with dark lashes. He had strong cheekbones and a square jaw, with a full mouth that stole her breath. "I'd never let anything happen to you."

Rain began to fall, cold and harsh, the January sky dark grey and ominous. But somehow as the carriage sped away, she'd never felt warmer or safer.

"Who are you?" she asked as she stared up at him, nearly hypnotized by the green flecks in his eyes.

His fingers splayed out on her back, his chin dropping close to her ear. "I'm the man who will always protect you. I promise you that. From now on, I will keep you safe."

What?

How could he make such a promise when they'd never even met?

The carriage slowed and Emily finally tore her gaze from his. Bash and another man approached on horseback. She drew in a quick, deep breath of air. But quickly released it again when one of his hands twined with hers.

Her gaze snapped back to his. "That doesn't tell me anything," she accused even as he lifted her hand to the handle on the back of the carriage and pushed her fingers around the bar.

"I wish I could tell you more."

"You can," she started to say but her words were lost as he jumped down from the carriage and darted into an alley.

Cold, hard wind bit through her pelisse as she watched him disappear. Never had a man affected her so and she didn't even know his name.

Want to read more? Duke of Dishonor

Want to read the entire series?
    Earl of Gold

Earl of Baxter
Duke of Decadence
Marquess of Menace
Duke of Dishonor
Baron of Blasphemy
Earl of Infamy
Viscount of Vanity
Laird of Longing

Keep up with all the latest news, sales, freebies, and releases by joining my newsletter!

www.tammyandresen.com

Hugs!

ABOUT THE AUTHOR

Tammy Andresen lives with her husband and three children just outside of Boston, Massachusetts. She grew up on the Seacoast of Maine, where she spent countless days dreaming up stories in blueberry fields and among the scrub pines that line the coast. Her mother loved to spin a yarn and Tammy filled many hours listening to her mother retell the classics. It was inevitable that at the age of eighteen, she headed off to Simmons College, where she studied English literature and education. She never left Massachusetts but some of her heart still resides in Maine and her family visits often.

Find out more about Tammy:
http://www.tammyandresen.com/
https://www.facebook.com/authortammyandresen
https://twitter.com/TammyAndresen
https://www.pinterest.com/tammy_andresen/
https://plus.google.com/+TammyAndresen/

OTHER TITLES BY TAMMY

Romancing the Rake

When only an Indecent Duke Will Do

How to Catch an Elusive Earl

Where to Woo a Bawdy Baron

When a Marauding Marquess is Best

What a Vulgar Viscount Needs

Who Wants a Brawling Baron

When to Dare a Dishonorable Duke

Lords of Scandal

Duke of Daring

Marquess of Malice

Earl of Exile

Viscount of Vice

Baron of Bad

Earl of Sin

The Wicked Wallflowers

Earl of Dryden

Too Wicked to Woo

Too Wicked to Wed

Too Wicked to Want

How to Reform a Rake

Don't Tell a Duke You Love Him

Meddle in a Marquess's Affairs

Never Trust an Errant Earl

Never Kiss an Earl at Midnight

Make a Viscount Beg

Wicked Lords of London

Earl of Sussex

My Duke's Seduction

My Duke's Deception

My Earl's Entrapment

My Duke's Desire

My Wicked Earl

Brethren of Stone

The Duke's Scottish Lass

Scottish Devil

Wicked Laird

Kilted Sin

Rogue Scot

The Fate of a Highland Rake

A Laird to Love

Christmastide with my Captain

My Enemy, My Earl

Heart of a Highlander

A Scot's Surrender

A Laird's Seduction

Taming the Duke's Heart

Taming a Duke's Reckless Heart

Taming a Duke's Wild Rose

Taming a Laird's Wild Lady

Taming a Rake into a Lord

Taming a Savage Gentleman

Taming a Rogue Earl

Fairfield Fairy Tales

Stealing a Lady's Heart

Hunting for a Lady's Heart

Entrapping a Lord's Love: Coming in February of 2018

American Historical Romance

Lily in Bloom

Midnight Magic

The Golden Rules of Love

Boxsets!!

Taming the Duke's Heart Books 1-3

American Brides

A Laird to Love

Wicked Lords of London

Printed in Great Britain
by Amazon